Praise for
Lady's Big Surprise

"In a world where horses are better than the mall, movies, or instant messaging, this story brings to life all the dreams that girls have about ponies. Young horse lovers will enjoy these adventures, which reinforce the magical connection between girls and horses."

~*Lynn Geiger,* ForeWord Magazine

"If you had told me that I would get wrapped up in *Lady's Big Surprise* I would have laughed wholeheartedly; but I did. In fact I read it cover to cover while on a camping trip and was amazed at the common sense horse-training references made throughout. This book is informative and genuinely entertaining. I am looking forward to the next one."

~*GaWANi Pony Boy*

"The book, first in a series, is compelling from the first sentence and leaves readers eagerly anticipating sequels."

~*Martha Barbone,* The Horse of Delaware Valley

Lady's Big Surprise

To Maia:

Happy trails!

J.M.D.

5-12-07

Books in the

STABLE SERIES

Book 1
Lady's Big Surprise
Hardback ISBN-13: 978-0-9746561-5-1
Paperback ISBN-13: 978-0-9746561-6-8

Book 2
Star of Wonder
Hardback ISBN-13: 978-0-9746561-3-7
Paperback ISBN-13: 978-0-9746561-4-4

Book 3
Willie to the Rescue
Hardback ISBN-13: 978-0-9746561-0-6
Paperback ISBN-13: 978-0-9746561-2-0

Book 4
Mary and Jody in the Movies
Hardback ISBN-13: 978-0-9746561-1-3
Paperback ISBN-13: 978-0-9746561-9-9

Lucky 1 Foot

BOOK 1 in THE LUCKY FOOT STABLE SERIES

Lady's Big Surprise

JoAnn S. Dawson

Lady's Big Surprise: Book 1 in the Lucky Foot Stable series
by JoAnn S. Dawson

Published by F. T. Richards Publishing — www.luckyfootseries.com.
Available to the trade from Biblio Distribution, Inc. Contact them at
800-462-6420 or visit their website at www.bibliodistribution.com.

Cover and interior illustration by Michelle Keenan
Lucky Foot Stable illustration by Tim Jackson
Cover and interior design by Pneuma Books, LLC
For more information, visit www.pneumabooks.com

Printed and bound in the United States of America
09 08 07 06 05   6 5 4 3 2

Publisher's Cataloging-in-Publication Data
(Prepared by The Donohue Group, Inc.)

Dawson, JoAnn S.
   Lady's big surprise / JoAnn S. Dawson.
      p. : ill. ; cm. -- (Lucky Foot Stable series ; Book 1)
      Hardcover ISBN-13: 978-0-9746561-5-1
      Hardcover ISBN-10: 0-9746561-5-1
      Softcover ISBN-13: 978-0-9746561-6-8
      Softcover ISBN-10: 0-9746561-6-X
1. Horses--Juvenile fiction.   2. Friendship--Juvenile fiction.   3.
Horses--Fiction.   4. Best friends--Fiction.   I. Title.

PS3554.A97 L33 2004
[Fic]   LCCN: 2003098084

To Mary, my epic friend

Lucky Foot Stable

Table of Contents

Table of Contents

1
Lucky Foot
Stable

"A HORSE SHOW! That's it! Why didn't I think of it before?" Mary shouted from her perch high on the bales of hay stacked in the loft of Lucky Foot Stable. Mary often went to the loft to think and was occasionally rewarded with a brilliant idea. "I've got to find Jody and see what she thinks! Come on, Finnegan!" She grabbed the knotty end of the creaky rope swing and swung herself down to the dirt floor, Finnegan the farm dog nipping at her heels and Colonel Sanders, the old white barn rooster, squawking indignantly at the uproar. Mary ran around to the side of the big white dairy barn and looked over the gate of the pasture field, where she could just make out Jody's form as she lay flat on her back on a horse blanket under the bare branches of the weeping willow tree.

"I knew that's where she'd be," laughed Mary. "I knew it, Finney!" and she flew across the pasture to share her latest great idea with Jody. Mary knew where Jody would be because Mary knew just about everything about Jody and her habits. Mary and Jody were friends. They weren't just good friends, or even best friends. They were, as Mary put it, "epic friends."

"Epic means: 'in the grand style, lofty in conception, and memorable!'" Mary liked to say. "I looked it up!"

Mary liked to say a lot of other things too. In fact, talking was one of Mary's favorite activities in the world, and Jody mostly liked to listen. But there were two things that brought them together and linked them forever ("never to be parted" they solemnly agreed) and best of all, gave them something to do together all through the long days of summer vacation and endless wintry weekends.

These two things were... the ponies! Mary's pony was the color of milk chocolate with a silky white mane and tail and four white stockings. Mary imagined that she had been born of a wild mustang and transported across the untamed plains by gypsies. So, when it came time to name the spunky mare, Mary solemnly touched the end of a riding crop gently to her shoulder and said, "I dub thee Gypsy Amber. *Gypsy* because it sounds romantic and *Amber* for the amber waves of grain on the plains!"

Jody contented herself with the original name of her pony, since everyone knows it's bad luck to change a pony's name. While not nearly as wild and mythical a name as Gypsy Amber, Jody didn't mind. Jody's pony was simply named Lady.

Lady was the color of copper pennies with uneven white patches over her withers, a small patch of white on her hindquarters, two white socks on her front legs, and a wiry black mane and tail. Of course, Mary took it upon herself to invent a story suitable for Lady's background.

"Lady was an Indian pony who used to hunt wild buffalo before coming here," Mary claimed. "Her name is really Lady White Cloud, because her patches look like clouds. And anyway, I'm sure the Indians always name their horses that way."

Jody just smiled at Mary's brilliance and continued to call the feisty mare Lady, Ladabucks, or sometimes just Lad.

"Jody Stafford, what in the world are you doing?" Mary asked with her hands on her hips, looking down at Jody looking up. "It's cold out here, isn't it?"

Jody pointed skyward at the lazy drift of the wispy clouds. "I'm watching the mare's tails and keeping Lady and Gypsy company, just like I always do. And when I get cold, I wrap up in the blanket. What are you doing?" Jody asked sweetly.

"I've been waiting in the stable for you to come in so I can tell you my great idea!"

"I didn't know you had a great idea, or I would've come in sooner," Jody said, sitting up and squinting into the sun. "What is it?"

"Well," Mary grinned, squatting down just enough so that Finnegan could lick her face. Finnegan was a herding dog — black and white with little brown patches over both eyes and a real talent for rounding up the cows at milking time. "Finney, quit it. Jody, remember how we've been practicing our jumping and our circus act with the ponies and wishing we could show off how great they are to an audience, but nobody ever sees us?" Mary asked, all in one breath.

"Yeah," Jody said expectantly.

"Well, all of a sudden it hit me — we can take the ponies to a horse show and enter some classes. Then everybody would see how great they are, and we would win all sorts of ribbons and trophies!"

Jody's hopeful expression suddenly fell at this pronouncement. "I don't know, Mare... we've never even been to a horse show, much less entered classes in one! We've just been stuck here on the farm, cantering around in the pasture, jumping logs and stuff."

"What about Secret Place?" Mary asked in a whisper, because the girls always whispered when they talked about Secret Place.

"Well, yeah," Jody said, "but it's still not anything like a horse show!"

"Jody, you'll see. You just leave it to me. We'll go get Willie and see if he'll take us to town to the feed store. That's where I've seen all the flyers about horse shows!" And off she flew across the pasture.

"But Willie's milking the cows! You know he doesn't like to be bothered when he's milking!" Jody yelled after her.

But Mary ran on, Finnegan yipping with excitement close behind.

The big pasture belonged to Mr. Robert McMurray, a very successful dairy farmer who didn't really like ponies all that much. But he had a little white horse stable with a green-shingled roof where the carriage horses used to be kept, and it wasn't very good for any other use. Jody's father often helped Mr. McMurray with building projects, so he generously allowed the girls to use the two stalls inside the stable. Mr. McMurray's ancient cowhand, Willie, had come up with the idea that if the cows ever got out of their pasture, Mary and Jody would be called upon to help Finnegan round them up with Lady and Gypsy — an exciting prospect indeed for the two girls, but one which so far, to their great disappointment, had not been necessary.

The girls named the little white barn Lucky Foot Stable because of the lucky white rabbit's foot they found inside one of the stalls while raking and sweeping them out on the first day. They promptly hung it over

"Jody, you always hang a horseshoe upside down to keep the luck from running out," Mary announced...

the stable door in the middle of an upside down horseshoe.

"Jody, you always hang a horseshoe upside down to keep the luck from running out," Mary had announced matter-of-factly while the girls swept and cleaned and painted and scrubbed until the little stable became a neat and cozy home for Lady and Gypsy Amber.

Now Mary ran as fast as she could past the open doors of Lucky Foot, around the corner, through the milk house, and into the dairy barn. The cows lifted their heads in alarm at the sight of her flying by in search of Willie.

"What the..." Willie exclaimed, unbending himself creakily from a cow's udder as Mary stopped dead, breathless.

"Willie, Willie! Do you remember the other day when you said you had to go to the feed store today to get some salt blocks for the cows?"

Willie scratched his ear with a gnarly finger. "I guess I said somethin' like that, why?"

"Well, me and Jody want to come with you. Can we, please?" Mary beseeched.

Willie bent over again to wash a cow's teat, thinking over the question, while Mary hopped from one foot to the other waiting for his reply. If there was one thing Mary knew about Willie, it was that he never answered anything too quickly and sometimes not at all. Finally Willie turned his head without having to stand up and strain his back. "I reckon there's room in the truck, if you go over and clear the front seat off."

"Oh, thank you, Willie! We'll clear it off the best ever!" she exclaimed, and out the door she ran, leaving Willie shaking his head as he put the milkers on another cow.

2
Willie's
Grand Plan

"Look, Jody, it's called a gymkhana. I can't wait to look that word up!" Mary exclaimed. The girls sat with their heads together on the front seat of Willie's old red pickup, trying to read the list of horse show classes between bumps in the road as Willie drove back to the farm from the feed store. "Listen to this: at Hilltop Farm, the first show of the season is on Saturday, February 13th — that's in two weeks! — promptly at 9:00 A.M. From the looks of this list, I'd say it just means a

13

whole bunch of games on horseback! Look, they have an obstacle course — Lady would beat the pants off all the other ponies in that class!"

Jody tried to hold the paper still as they jounced over the rough road. "What about this? 'Keyhole race!' Gypsy is so fast — she could win that easily!"

"Look! Bobbing for apples, sack race, and egg in spoon — I wonder what you have to do for that one?" Mary went on. "This is going to be so fun!"

Willie glanced out of the corner of his eye at the two girls poring over the list of classes and scratched his head.

"Seems awful early in the year for a horse show," he commented. "Better hope for a nice day. And how do you reckon you're gonna get yourselves to that... gym... gym... what in the heck is that thing called again?"

"A gymkhana, Willie!" cried Mary. "And it's true, we haven't quite figured that out yet."

"Maybe we could ride there," Jody offered.

"Are you crazy, girl?" Willie harrumphed. "Hilltop Farm is at least twenty miles away."

"We could ride halfway one day and camp overnight in the woods, and ride the rest of the way the next day!" Mary said optimistically. "We could bring Finnegan to protect us overnight!"

"Where in tarnation do you two get such far-fetched notions in your noggins?" Willie snorted. "First, that dog would just as soon lick somebody to death as protect you from them, and second, it's too cold to camp overnight in the woods, and last, you can't ride no twenty miles to no horse show. Why, by the time you got there, them ponies'd be so dragged out they'd keel over dead in the first contest!"

"Well, there must be some way," Jody said dejectedly.

"We'll have to figure it out when we get back to Lucky Foot," Mary announced.

"Here it is, Jody! 'gymkhana: a place
for athletic games — a sports meet.'"

Willie glanced at the two suddenly downhearted girls and furrowed his brow in thought. A moment later a hint of a smile played around his mouth, and he actually stepped a little harder on the gas, exceeding his normal speed of twenty five miles per hour.

Back at Lucky Foot Stable, Mary and Jody sat on a bale of straw, Finnegan sleeping at their feet and Colonel Sanders peering down at them from his roosting spot on the top board of Lady's stall. Colonel Sanders spent much of his time strutting around the farm, clucking and scratching and making sure everyone knew he was the boss, but when he needed a rest or some company, he headed for Lucky Foot Stable.

The ponies hung their heads over the stall doors, watching as Jody read over the list of gymkhana classes once again while Mary turned the pages of her well-worn dictionary to the letter g.

"Here it is, Jody! '*gymkhana*: a place for athletic games — a sports meet.'"

"Does it say anything about horses?" Jody asked.

"No, but it means games."

"Well, I can see that from the list, Mare. Now if you could just find something in that dictionary of yours that tells us how to get the horses there!'"

"We'll just have to figure that out," Mary stated.

Just then, Willie appeared in the stable doorway, tugging on his ear lobe the way he always did when he was thinking hard about something.

"Willie!" Mary exclaimed, "listen to this!" and she read the definition of gymkhana to him. "What do you think of that?"

"I think it's all a pipe dream unless you got some way to get yourselves there," he replied flatly.

"Oh, we're going to work on that next," Mary declared.

"Well, now, I've been thinkin' on it," Willie said carefully. "I figure maybe we could fix somethin' up on the back of the pickup somehow..."

Mary jumped off the bale before Willie could finish his sentence. "Willie! Do you mean we could haul the ponies in the back of the truck? Would that work? Is that really possible?"

Willie tugged even harder on his ear lobe. "Well, there is one problem with it... when you say ponies..."

Mary and Jody looked at each other.

"What do you mean, Willie?" Jody asked.

"Now, now... maybe it's a bad idea all the way around," Willie replied.

"No, Willie, just tell us what you're thinking," Mary prodded.

"Well, I figure we could put some sides on the pickup and tie up a pony in the back..."

"A pony?" asked Jody. "You mean, just one pony?"

"Now, I can't figure how we could fit more than one back there. The bed of the truck just ain't wide enough for two. So, you see…"

"Willie, are you sure? We haven't tried it before. Maybe there's more room than you think," Jody commented hopefully.

"No, Jody… Willie's right. Putting one pony back there is going to be hard enough. So, it's decided then," Mary said matter-of-factly.

Now it was Willie and Jody who looked at each other.

"What do you mean, Mary?" asked Jody.

"She means it was a bad idea all the way around," said Willie. "I knew it was. You girls will just have to stay home here and have your own gymkhana out in the pasture field." Willie had pronounced *gymkhana* like *gym-canna*, and it took some effort for Mary to restrain herself from correcting him.

"No, Willie, that's not what I meant. I meant we can take one pony," Mary continued.

This suggestion was greeted with a silence that filled the little stable until Finnegan, sensing something amiss, raised his head and whined and Lady nickered softly from her stall.

"But... but, Mary, Lady would be so lonely back here without Gypsy for the day," Jody sputtered.

"Who said anything about Gypsy going?" Mary giggled. "It would be Lady who would go, of course. You and Lady, and I will be your groom. Now, Willie, when can we start putting the sides on the truck?"

"Mary! I can't go without you!" Jody protested. "Why would Lady go instead of Gypsy? Willie, what is she talking about?" Jody turned to Willie.

But Willie didn't answer. He just stood in the doorway with a half smile on his face as he watched the two girls.

"Jody, you're not going without me. I just said I would be your groom. And Lady is going instead of Gypsy simply because she is the better gymkhana pony. No offense, Gypsy," Mary said quickly to her pony, who didn't look offended in the least. "Lady has proven it many times while practicing our circus act and on trips to Secret Place. Now, with a little more practice, Gypsy could improve, and maybe she'll go next time."

Mary jumped from her bale and turned to Jody, who sat with her mouth hanging open in shock.

"Come on, time's a wastin'! Jody, shut your mouth and get up so we can help Willie figure out how to put the sides on the truck." And with that she was gone before Willie or Jody could reply.

3
Loading Up

THE GIRLS SPENT most of the next two weeks helping Willie design and build the wooden sides for the old red pickup truck between milkings, and now it was ready for a test. Willie had backed the truck up with the tailgate down so that it rested on the barn hill. That way Lady could just walk right in without having to step up.

"Now, Lady, don't mind that it isn't a real trailer. It's just as good, and sturdier really, since the wheels are right under you holding you up," Mary said reassuringly as she led the mare up to the makeshift trailer. The girls smiled with pride at the painted white sides and the thick bed of straw covering the bed and tailgate. Lady responded by putting her head down immediately to graze, ignoring the truck altogether.

"All you have to do is get in like a good girl, and we'll be off to the gymkhana, where you'll win all sorts of ribbons and trophies and things," Mary continued, pulling Lady's head up and trying to get her to at least sniff the truck.

"Oh, Mare, do you really think she'll get in?" Jody asked nervously. "It must look awfully scary to a pony, especially the first..."

"Of course she'll get in!" Mary interrupted loudly, nudging Jody with her elbow. "Don't say anything to get her worried!" she whispered fiercely in Jody's ear. "Now, just wait — I'm going to go get Gypsy so she can watch."

It was Mary's theory that Gypsy should be

there when Lady stepped into the truck, so that Gypsy would know what to do when her time came.

Just as Mary returned with Gypsy in tow, Willie came hobbling from the other side of the barn, having finished the milking.

"Willie," Mary called, "we're ready whenever you are! Lady is as cool as a cucumber!"

"Mary, Lady doesn't even know what's going on yet," Jody reminded her, leading the pony around the pickup to get her used to being near it. "She thinks we're just out for a stroll."

Willie took off his hat and scratched his head for a moment before speaking. "Now, Jody, what you have to do is just lead her on like nothin' out of the ordinary is goin' on. Don't make a big fuss about it, or she'll start gettin' nervous-like. Next time you go around the truck, lead her away a little, and then just walk her on like nobody's business. Don't give her a chance to think about what's happenin'."

"Why, Willie, I thought you only knew about cows," Mary said with new respect. "You sound like you've done this before!"

Willie tugged his ear thoughtfully. "I've had a horse or two in my day, young lady. Used to ride a great big gray field horse named Dapples. He stepped on my foot once when I was a young'un. Had to bite him on the shoulder to get him off."

Mary wanted to ask more about the field horse, but Willie was concentrating on the matter at hand. "Now, Jody," he continued without missing a beat, "lead her out a little way further. That's it; now turn and lead her right in, but don't hold her so short. Give her some rope and kind of let her feel her way in."

Jody did as she was told, leading Lady a little bit away from the truck and giving her some rope. Then, turning her around as if nothing out of the ordinary was happening, she walked resolutely to the open tailgate with Lady in tow.

"That's it, Jody. Now just walk right on!" Willie instructed from the sidelines.

Jody walked onto the tailgate and was halfway into the bed of the truck, Lady following easily behind until her front hooves hit the metal tailgate that was so carefully hidden under the bed of straw. To Lady, this did not feel or sound at all like her stall floor with its packed dirt footing — it was hard and clanky and made an awful noise through the straw when she put her weight on it!

"Look out, Jode!" Mary yelled as Lady showed her displeasure by jerking her head up and rearing back just far enough to get off the tailgate, pulling Jody along with her until she stood on the barn hill, snorting and pawing in confusion.

"Lady! Where are your manners?" Mary cried, not being able to do much else, since she had Gypsy in hand. "You're not setting a very good example!"

"What should we do now, Willie?" Jody asked, patting Lady to calm her down.

"Well," Willie answered thoughtfully, "I kinda figured she might pull that trick the first time. They don't like it when they feel somethin' different like that underfoot. And she's never had to get in the back of an old truck before. Have you, old girl?" Willie turned to Lady, patting her reassuringly. "Now, we have to try her again. This time just lead her up and let her sniff around a little till she gets more used to the idea."

"Willie, wouldn't it help if we put some hay in front, and maybe some grain? She might smell it and get on to eat!" Mary suggested. "We know Lady loves to eat — it's her favorite pastime!"

"I reckon we could do that. I was going to wait till tomorrow to rig up a hay net, but you could just lay a flake of hay in the front there with a little mound of grain on top of it. That might encourage her a little."

"I'll get it!" Mary yelled, handing Gypsy's lead rope to Willie and running around the side of the barn to the horse stable. Almost before Willie realized he was left holding the pony, Mary was back with a flake of hay and a handful of grain. She laid the hay down carefully in the front of the truck bed, placing the small mound of grain on top.

"There you are, Lad... now that's more interesting!" she assured the mare as she took Gypsy's rope from Willie's grasp. And sure enough, Lady extended her muzzle toward the grain, sniffing and even taking a tiny step toward the tailgate.

"Yep, she's thinkin' about goin' on," Willie said confidently. "Now, Mary, you just go tie Gypsy up to the fence there and come back here and help me. We have to get her on this time, or she'll start figurin' that she can outsmart us."

Mary did as she was told and was back to the truck in a flash. Lady took another step toward the tailgate, definitely interested in the grain inside. Another few steps and she would be on it again. Jody stood patiently

Lady took another step toward the tailgate, snorting quietly as she extended her muzzle to sniff the straw.

by her side, holding the rope and letting Lady sniff the ground just in front of the tailgate.

"OK, now Mary, get behind here and take hold of my wrist, and I'm going to take hold of yours, and with our arms locked, we're gonna push her from behind while Jody leads her on again. But first, Jody, see if you can just pull her up real gentle-like another little step or two. I don't think she's too afraid now."

"Come on, Lady..." Jody said softly. "Don't be scared. See that nice grain up there?" All the while she tugged gently on the lead, and Lady took another step toward the tailgate, snorting quietly as she extended her muzzle to sniff the straw.

"That's it," said Willie in a low voice. "She's losin' her fear, and she's eyein' that grain. Now, Jody, be a little firmer. We're gonna push. Everybody work together and don't let her think about it too much. As soon as she starts goin' in, Mary, we have to push as hard as we can 'fore she changes her mind."

"Ready, Willie!" whispered Mary gleefully, while Jody bit her fingernails.

"Willie, what if she won't go?"

"Don't worry, Jody, if you do your job and pull her on she'll go. Now give her a little rope again, because the shorter you hold her head, the more she'll want to pull back. Just let her think it's her idea to go on and eat that grain. You go on up into the bed and pull and we'll push. Ready?"

"I guess!" Jody said. "Come on, Lady!" she encouraged as she went up into the bed and pulled.

"Go!" Willie yelled to Mary, and they pushed. And before Lady knew what was happening, she was on the truck, and Willie had the tailgate up and the rear panel tied to the side panels.

"Good girl! Good girl!" Jody exclaimed, patting Lady furiously on the neck, relieved that she had gone on with only two tries. "Now you can have your grain!"

"Thanks ever so, Willie!" Mary cried.

"Gypsy, did you see that? Now don't let me catch you giving us any trouble when your turn comes!"

Gypsy, of course, was still tied to the fence and hadn't a clue what had transpired.

"Now don't get too cocky," Willie said. "We'll have to practice puttin' her on and off a few times, just so we know she'll load tomorrow."

Lady, once on the truck and realizing there was not much she could do about escaping, snorted just once more for effect and then began nibbling contentedly on the grain and hay on the floor of her makeshift trailer.

4
Off to the Show

THE NEXT DAY dawned sunny and brisk,
not too cold for February, really a perfect
day for a horse show. Lady and Gypsy
watched curiously from their stalls as the
girls bustled around Lucky Foot Stable gathering the supplies they would need for the
show — hard brushes, soft brushes, mane
and tail combs, a hoof pick, a water bucket,
lead ropes, a shovel, Jody's riding helmet,
and Lady's new bridle.

"I'm so glad I asked my dad for this little

tack box last Christmas!" Jody said. "It holds all the stuff we need to take to the horse show perfectly!"

They had already groomed Lady from head to toe, more thoroughly than ever before, so as to make a good impression on the judges.

"Now, Jody, you should be sitting down, preparing yourself mentally for the show, as I am your groom and I should be doing all the stuff the groom is supposed to do," Mary declared rather pompously as she scrubbed two brushes together to get the dust out.

"Mary, don't be ridiculous," Jody answered, putting the finishing touches on her bridle with a sponge and leather conditioner. "Besides, if I think about the show too much, I'll get so nervous I won't go at all. Oh, I wish you and Gypsy were riding too!"

"Well, next time we'll ride. Then I'll be the nervous one, and you can tell *me* to sit down," Mary said.

"Mare, do you think we should give

Lady a bath?" Jody worried, examining Lady's coat carefully for any dirt or dust that may have been left behind. "I think all the big show people always bathe their horses before a show."

"Well, that's because all the big show people have big beautiful wash stalls where they have hot and cold running water and hoses and things and they can cross-tie their horses, and it's really easy. Now, we'd have to get out a bunch of buckets and mix the hot and cold water from the barn and have a soapy mix in some and the rinse water in others, and then we'd have to use a lot of towels to dry her off and she might not dry in time for the show anyway. But, we can do it if you want," she finished sweetly, like a good groom.

"Well, I didn't think of all that," Jody replied. "I guess she's clean enough as she is."

"Besides, it doesn't matter, because she's going to be so much better than the others at all the games that she'd win even if she was covered with mud!" Mary stated confidently.

"I wish I was as sure as you are, Mary. We've never done this before."

"You'll be great, I tell you," Mary said. "Now I'm going to go get Willie. He should be done milking by now. He can help us load. I'll carry the tack box around and put it in the truck."

"I'll get the grain and hay," Jody volunteered.

Mary went around to the barn to fetch Willie while Jody carried the flake of hay and the grain over to the barn hill where the truck sat waiting for its passenger. The tailgate was down and ready, and Jody had just arranged the hay with the grain on top when Willie and Mary appeared.

"I'll go get Lady!" Mary said excitedly. "That's the groom's job!"

"You can go get her, but you let Jody load her, just like yesterday. We don't want nothin' different gettin' her upset," Willie ordered.

"I will, I will, I will, Willie!" Mary yelled over her shoulder as she ran off to get Lady from her stall.

"She's more excited than you, ain't she?" Willie asked Jody with a smile and a shake of his head.

"Oh, Willie, that's because she doesn't have anything to be nervous about. Do you think Lady will load OK?"

"I don't see why she wouldn't. You two loaded her and unloaded her 'bout ten times yesterday, didn't you?"

"Mary got a little carried away," Jody giggled as Mary came running up to the barn hill, Lady trotting behind.

"Here you go, Jode! Now don't forget what we practiced yesterday!"

"Don't worry, Mare. How could I possibly?" she said, taking Lady's lead and guiding her smoothly onto the tailgate and into the bed of the truck, where she immediately dropped her head and began eating the grain. Willie closed up the back and fastened the panels together while Jody cross-tied the mare securely with slip knots. Then she climbed neatly out of the bed of the truck and, after checking to make sure nothing was forgotten, the trio was off to the show.

The long ride to the gymkhana seemed even longer due to the uneasy and unusual silence of the two girls, each thinking her own thoughts and unwilling to share them. Willie drove in silence as well, glancing at them occasionally while keeping an eye on Lady balancing herself in the bed of the pickup. The silence was broken only when Mary spotted the large red and white sign reading "Horse Show" that was posted at the side of the road.

"Look, Willie! There it is!" she screeched. "Turn here!"

"I see it, girl, I see it," Willie answered patiently, turning into the long lane leading to the show grounds. "Looks like quite a few horses turned out."

"Oh, no," groaned Jody at the sight of the number of horse trailers parked in the open field along the lane. "Mary, there's a million horses here. We don't stand a chance!"

"Oh, Jody, don't be silly. There's not one horse or pony here that compares to Lady. You'll see." Mary said confidently. "Wow, look. They have an outdoor ring and an indoor ring! And, Jody! Look at the horses out in the field behind the barn! They must live here. Aren't they gorgeous? Look at that black one with the white star! He's all by himself in that paddock — he must be the Black Stallion!" she giggled.

No reply came from Jody as she struggled to swallow the lump of fear that had traveled suddenly from her stomach to her throat. She pointed wordlessly at the trailers, some large and some small, but all real trailers nonetheless. There was not one other pickup truck with a pony riding in the back. And what was worse, it seemed everyone was staring at Lady as Willie drove around in search of a parking space.

"Well, you must admit we have the most interesting mode of transportation!" Mary observed gleefully while Jody sunk lower in her seat. "There's a spot, Willie!" she continued, pointing to a space next to a beautiful red and white trailer with a matching truck.

"I see it, Mary, but I've gotta find a high place like the barn hill so we can back up to it. That way Lady won't have to back out into thin air. She needs to feel the ground under her feet when we unload her. Then we can park. And I think I see just the spot right over there." Willie indicated a gentle rise in the grass near the outdoor riding ring, where several horses were already warming up for the games. "We'll back up over there and get her out."

"But, Willie, everyone will be watching!"

Jody protested, having found her voice at last.

"Well, if you got a better suggestion, you better let me know now. Do you want your pony falling out the back of the truck?"

"No," Jody squeaked, ashamed of herself for worrying about what everyone would think.

"C'mon, Jode, let's get out and guide Willie back to the hill," Mary said sympathetically. "Don't worry about what everybody thinks," she whispered. "Just remember, Lady's the best." And she squeezed Jody's arm.

Willie backed easily to the grassy rise and took down the rear panel of the makeshift trailer. Jody climbed into the bed of the truck, untied Lady, and with a gentle push on her chest, guided her out of the truck just as she had done on the barn hill at home.

"Did you see that?" Mary yelled to no one in particular. "Nothin' to it!"

"Mary, not so loud," Jody pleaded. "We're

already attracting enough attention." And it was true. The riders in the ring had stopped warming up their horses to watch the curious unloading from the truck bed.

"Quit yer gabbin' now and get that pony ready for her first class," Willie reminded the girls sternly. "I'll park the truck over by that red trailer. You trot Lady around some to get the kinks out of her legs, then bring her over to the truck and get her cleaned up and bridled."

At that, Mary sprang into action. "Jody, you get her bridle. I'll get the grooming stuff. After all, I am the groom!" she laughed.

The girls were at the truck the minute Willie parked it. Mary got out the brushes and combs and groomed Lady vigorously from head to toe until her red and white coat shone and her mane and tail glistened in the sun. Knowing something special was about to happen, Lady snorted and stamped her foot, nudging Jody impatiently with her muzzle.

"Hold on, Lady. I'm just fixin' up your bridle," Jody giggled, buffing the dark leather with a soft cloth and a touch of neat's-foot oil.

"You ain't goin' to need your bridle if you don't hurry up and enter your classes," Willie prodded from his seat on the tailgate of the truck. "You been brushin' and cleanin' and buffin' long enough."

"You're right, Willie!" Mary exclaimed. "Jody, bridle up while I go over to the show secretary and enter you in your classes and get your number."

"Mary, are you sure you know what I want to enter?" Jody asked nervously.

"I guess I do! We circled the classes on the list back at the barn, and I brought it with me! Keyhole race, obstacle course, dollar bareback, and pole bending. Will you relax? I'll be right back!"

Jody bridled Lady, and Willie gave her a leg up so that she could warm up with the other horses in the ring. As she and Lady

47

entered through the gate, the other riders looked her way, and she began to feel more confident. She was sure they must be admiring the beauty of her pony, the only pinto in the ring among all of the chestnuts, bays, and grays. As Jody nudged Lady into a trot, Mary returned from the entry booth waving her number in the air.

"Jody!" she yelled from the sidelines. "I got it! You're entered!"

Jody smiled in spite of her embarassment and rode to the rail, leaning over to take her number from Mary.

"Number thirty-four. I hope it's a lucky number!" Jody exclaimed.

"Well, I heard somebody at the entry booth talking about the judge," Mary whispered loudly. "They say he's really hard to please, and not only that, he's not very nice!"

"Oh, great! Why did you have to tell me that, Mary? Are you trying to make me even more nervous?

"No, I'm trying to tell you that he's going

to love Lady because she is eager to please, and he'll be able to see that," Mary said confidently.

Before Jody could answer, a girl with long braids flowing down her back from beneath her riding helmet rode up on a big beautiful chestnut mare and halted alongside Lady.

"I like your pony," she said. "What's her name?"

"Oh, it's just Lady," Jody said shyly.

"Are you warming up for dollar bareback already?" the girl continued. "It's not till the end of the day, you know."

"No, I'm just warming up in general," Jody said.

"Well, didn't you forget something?" the girl asked, staring pointedly at Lady's back.

Just then a man called out sharply to the girl from across the ring. "Janelle, come on. You're wasting time."

"That's my trainer. I've got to go. Well, good luck," she said, but not very sincerely.

"Are you warming up for dollar bareback already?
It's not till the end of the day, you know."

As the girl turned and trotted away, Jody looked down at Lady's back, looked at Mary and Willie, then stared around the ring at all the other horses before whispering to Mary in a sudden panic.

"Mare... I don't have a saddle! Everybody else has a saddle! I was so nervous... I just noticed... everybody has a saddle but us! What should I do?"

"What do you mean, what should you do?" Mary exclaimed. "You can ride without one! It didn't say anything on the show list about having a saddle!"

"But that's probably because everybody automatically knew you have to have one! We have to go home!" she cried. And she jumped off of Lady right there in the ring.

Mary was just opening her mouth when Willie stepped in.

"Jody, you get yourself right back up on that pony's back and let me go see about it. Mary's right. Just because everybody else has a saddle, that don't mean you have to. It's just games, not jumpin' fences or anything. And it didn't say nothin' about it in the rules, so if you don't have one, I don't see how they can make a fuss about it."

Mortified beyond words, Jody obeyed Willie and jumped nimbly onto Lady's back, heading straight out of the ring before anyone else might have the chance to talk to her. Mary met her at the gate.

"Jody, if that show committee has any sense, they'll let you ride, because everybody knows the best way to learn your balance is riding bareback. And this is just a gymkhana. It's not like a regular show, and if they let you ride, you're going to win everything. So you just go ahead and demonstrate your riding ability, which is way better than anybody else's here. You don't need a dumb old unnecessary saddle!"

"But, Mary, we should have known we had to have a saddle! I know we always ride bareback at home, but nobody ever rides bareback in a show! We were just

being stupid! Everybody's going to laugh!"
And she covered her face in dismay.

5
The Obstacle Course

Finally arriving at the front of the line at the entry booth, Willie found himself face to face with two large women wearing wide-brimmed straw hats and sitting behind a table, their pencils poised over the entry form.

"May I help you?" said one, smiling sweetly.

"Well, ma'am, my rider's already entered," said Willie, taking off his hat respectfully. "We just wanted to let you know that we'll be ridin' today without a saddle in all the classes, not just dollar bareback. Didn't want to cause no surprises for the judges."

One woman's mouth dropped open as she looked at Willie, then past him at the ring beyond, then at the woman sitting beside her, who looked back with her mouth just as wide. Finally she found her voice.

"No saddle?" she asked simply.

"No, ma'am," Willie answered, tugging on his ear lobe.

"But... but... this is highly irregular! We allow either western or English saddles, but no saddle at all? I don't know how we can possibly..."

Well, ma'am, the way I see it, there's nothin' in your rules here about a saddle," Willie interrupted, holding up the list of classes, "and everybody knows the way to learn your balance is to start off bareback. My rider over there can probably ride better bareback than any of your riders here with all their fancy equipment. Now if you can find some good reason why I have to go back over there and tell that little girl she has to pack up her pony and go home, then you better let me know what it is. Otherwise, I'll be goin' back now to help her git ready for her first class." Willie stood waiting for her reply, his hat in his hand.

"Well!" the woman huffed, glancing once again at the other woman, who was smiling at Willie in spite of herself. Seeing no help from that direction, she addressed Willie again.

"Well! This is highly irregular!" she said once more, for lack of a better comment. "Sir, I myself will allow it, but I must take it under advisement with the judge, and if he rules differently, I must comply with his ruling."

"Yes, ma'am. I appreciate that. And if he says different, you just send somebody right over there to those two girls groomin' that pretty little pinto pony and let them know they have to go home after spendin' all that time with their hearts set on goin' to their very first horse show."

And Willie put on his hat, tipped it to

the woman, and turned to help Jody get ready for her first class. She watched him go with her mouth open, speechless.

"What'd she say, Willie? What'd she say?" Mary asked impatiently as Willie approached. Jody was too upset to ask, silently hoping she said no.

"She said to git your bridle on and git over to the ring before you miss your class," Willie replied sternly.

"Oh, goody! What did I tell you, Jody?" Mary said gleefully. "Let's go!"

"What is my first class?" Jody asked miserably.

"Now, look here," Willie said, seeing Jody's dismay. "You're here to do your best and have a good time. This is a fun show, and you're s'posed to have fun. Now wipe that long look off yer face and git up on that pony and show her off for all she's worth. And don't worry about winnin', just worry about doin' your best."

"Winning wouldn't hurt either," Mary

whispered, as she gave Jody a leg up. "Your first class is the obstacle course!" she continued loudly. "This will be Lady's best event! She's not scared of anything! They're going over to the ring now. Come on! And, Jody, just look at Lady! She *knows* she's at a show. She *is* showing herself off for all she's worth!"

And it was true. Lady was snorting and prancing, tossing her head and tail, her nostrils flaring as she trotted over to the ring. Jody couldn't help but sit up and smile proudly, suddenly remembering that her pony was the best at the show.

Mary and Willie stood near the gate as Jody and Lady approached show ring one, where the obstacles were set up for the first class. The announcer's voice came clearly over the speaker positioned at the very top of a telephone pole beside the ring.

"Good morning and welcome to the Games on Horseback at Hilltop Farm! Our judge today is Mr. John Hannum, and our ringmaster is Reggie Brown. Our first class of the day is the obstacle course, and we have eight entries. If you are in class number one, please be ready at the gate and study your course chart."

"Here she comes," Mary whispered to Willie as Lady pranced to the gate. "Isn't she gorgeous?"

But Willie's attention was drawn to a conversation taking place in the center of the ring between the show secretary and the judge. The red-faced woman was waving her hands, holding up the show list, and pointing first at Willie, then at Jody and Lady. The judge looked at the list, listened to the woman, and then finally looked at the nervous girl outside the gate on the prancing pinto pony. And then he walked over and leaned over the top rail to talk to Jody.

"What's going on? What's he saying? I heard he's not very nice, you know. I'm going over there. The groom needs to know what's happening," Mary said all in one breath to Willie.

"You just stay put right where you are," said Willie wisely, grabbing Mary's arm and holding her in place. "Jody can handle this situation herself."

So Mary could only watch in a small huff as the judge talked to Jody.

"What's your name, young lady?" the judge asked sternly.

"My name?" asked Jody, her voice quavering as she glanced around at the other riders, who had all stopped to watch. "Um, my name is Jody."

"And the name of your pony?"

"Oh, it's Lady, sir, just Lady," she answered, patting Lady's neck nervously.

"Hmph," said the judge, rubbing his chin. He stood looking at Lady for what seemed like an hour, then patted her on the shoulder. "That's a nice simple name. Easy to remember," he said finally. "I had a pony something like her when I was about your age."

"Really?" Jody exclaimed, forgetting her nervousness for a second.

"Now, what about your saddle, Jody? Did you not think it was necessary to bring one for a gymkhana?"

Jody's mouth opened but no words came as she felt her face getting hot. She knew that she was flushing beet red as the judge waited for her answer. "I... I..."

The judge moved closer and lowered his voice almost to a whisper. "Do you have a saddle, young lady?"

Jody lowered her eyes to the ground, shook her head miserably, and finally managed a weak, "no," ready to flee in the next instant. But then the judge patted her hand.

"That's all right, Jody. When I was your age, I didn't have a saddle either. I learned to ride bareback, and it was the best thing I ever did. No better way to learn your balance and strength. Made it to the Armed Forces Cavalry Division because of it. Now, I'm going to allow you to ride today, even though it's not quite normal, but next time you'll know that everybody else rides in a saddle at a horse show. It's probably best if you do too, so as to not cause any fuss with the show committee. You know what I mean?" And he winked at Jody as if they were old friends.

"Yes, sir. Thank you, sir," Jody smiled, holding her head high and patting Lady proudly on the shoulder.

"Now, take your place at the gate and let's get started."

Jody rode Lady to the fence rail where Mary and Willie waited anxiously and leaned over to whisper, "Mare! The judge is so nice!" before she and Lady pranced away to wait their turn at the gate for the obstacle course.

As the judge passed the fence on his way to the judge's platform, he glanced over at Willie with a sudden look of recognition.

"William!" he smiled in surprise, giving Willie a salute, "How are you? Haven't seen you in years! I'll have to talk to you later."

Willie nodded and saluted back as the judge continued to his platform. Mary, speechless for one of the few times in her life, stared at Willie, her mouth hanging open in shock.

"Willie! You know the judge!" she finally exclaimed.

"Yep, we rode together years ago," Willie said, and he didn't say any more.

"But you never told us you used to ride, except the old plow horses on the farm," Mary prodded.

"Hush up now. The ringmaster is explainin' the course," Willie said, ignoring Mary by turning his full attention to the goings-on in the ring. And Mary had no choice but to do the same.

The ringmaster stood in the middle of the ring, course chart in hand, speaking through a bullhorn so that everyone could hear.

"Riders, listen carefully. I will only explain the course once!" he said importantly. "First, you will dismount and enter through the gate leading your horse, then mount up. The first obstacle you will encounter is the wooden bridge. You must walk your horse over the bridge."

And the ringmaster walked himself over the bridge, which was a flat pallet covered with a piece of plywood and flanked by two white jump standards.

"That's just like the wooden bridge at Secret Place, only the one at Secret Place is way scarier, over real water and everything," Mary whispered to Willie. "Lady won't mind that at all."

"Next you must trot over the trotting poles (these were wooden rails placed about a foot apart on the ground) and jump the bales of straw."

"We've done that a million times at the barn," Mary said, louder this time. "Those bales aren't even that high, because they're laying flat instead of up on their sides, like we put them at home. They are a little wider, though, but Lady can do it."

Willie just smiled.

"Next, you must walk your horse over the

sheet of plastic!" shouted the ringmaster, demonstrating by walking over it himself. The plastic was about four feet wide, stretched out on the ground, and held down by two wooden rails on either side.

"Lady won't mind that," Mary giggled.

"And then, you must trot in and out around the barrels, and at the last barrel, pick up the egg on the spoon and carry it to the next obstacle."

The barrels were standing on end, placed rather closely together so that the riders would have to steer their horses carefully around them to avoid knocking them over.

"We do that all the time at home, in and out of the old fence posts," Mary commented. "And Lady is such a smooth walker, Jody won't drop the egg. No way!" she continued.

"Will you just hush up a minute so I can hear what he's sayin'?" Willie said in exasperation.

"Sorry, Willie."

"And next," the ringmaster continued,

"you will pick up the umbrella from the fence, open it, then shut it, and place it back on the fence."

"Uh-oh, that's one thing Lady's never had to do. Who would be dumb enough to ride in the rain, anyway? I don't know if she's going to like that one!" Mary worried.

"Next you will pick up the jugs from this fencepost and carry them forward to the third marked post," the ringmaster continued. "And please, if your horse spooks at the jugs, just drop them! We don't want anyone getting hurt!"

Mary kept quiet this time, but she secretly smiled as she looked at the three plastic jugs tied together, knowing that Lady was used to Jody carrying all sorts of things on her back, and she never spooked at any of them.

"Finally, you will canter over to the gate, halt, open the gate while mounted, walk through, and then shut and latch it from the other side, also still mounted."

At this, Mary laughed out loud. "We do

that all the time at home too, because we're too lazy to get off and open the gates!"

"Now, for the last time, hush, the first horse is goin' in!" admonished Willie.

The first horse to go in was the big chestnut ridden by the girl with the long braids. The girl led him quietly through the gate and mounted up smoothly just inside, as the ringmaster had instructed. Then she rode him over the bridge without a hitch. He trotted easily over the trotting poles and hopped over the bales of straw as the girl smiled smugly.

"Uh-oh, Willie, this one is pretty good," Mary whispered.

The chestnut walked up to the sheet of plastic confidently enough, but when he set one hoof on it and it crinkled and moved, he jumped back and snorted, pawing the ground in fear.

"Uh-oh!" Mary exclaimed without thinking, loudly enough for several people along the rail to turn and look at her.

"Mary, you've got to keep your mouth

shut!" Willie warned. "Clap your hand over it if you have to."

Mary, feeling foolish at her outburst, dutifully clapped her hand over her mouth as the chestnut continued the course.

The girl was kicking him forward now, as he lowered his head and snorted again at the plastic. He took a step forward, and a step back, and another forward. Finally he gathered himself up and jumped neatly over the whole piece of plastic, which was really quite a big jump.

"Oh!" Mary gasped through her hand. But it didn't matter because a lot of other people were gasping too, as the girl tried to keep her seat after the jump, which had taken her completely by surprise. The judge was at her side in an instant, grasping the calf of her leg to help her stay on.

"I'm fine!" the girl said angrily through her embarrassment. "I'll finish the course."

As the judge stepped back, she gripped her crop in her hand and began whacking the horse over and over on his rump, jerking on his mouth, and turning him in circles as she did so.

"Now go on!" she ordered, as she straightened him out and trotted him, his muscles trembling with fear, toward the barrels. Mary's mouth made a big round *o* as she unclapped her hand, but no sound came out. Willie shook his head in disgust and said under his breath, "Take care of that, John."

As if the judge heard Willie's comment, he stepped in front of the girl before she made it halfway to the barrels and held up his hand for her to halt. Although Mary and Willie were all the way on the other side of the ring, they could hear the judge's words clearly.

"Young lady, I'm going to allow you to finish the course because it's good training for your horse," he said evenly. "But if I see another display like the one I just saw from you, you'll be disqualified not only from this ring but for the rest of the day. Do you understand me?"

The girl looked down red faced and haughty at the judge, as scattered applause came from the crowd at his words. Then her attention was drawn to her trainer, who had opened the gate and was making sharp gestures for her to exit the ring. With one last jerk on the chestnut's mouth, she trotted him to the gate as the trainer commented loudly enough for the judge and everyone else to hear.

"You did fine, Janelle. The horse needed that. But we don't need this rinky-dink, two-bit show with a judge who doesn't understand discipline. We'll take you out of the rest of the day so he won't have the chance to disqualify you."

And as everyone watched, she trotted away with her head in the air, the trainer close behind, to scratch the rest of her classes.

Mary stood dumbfounded at all that had

taken place, but she soon found her voice, as she always did.

"Willie, can you believe that? I thought the trainer was going to yell at her for that, but he told her she did the right thing! Can you believe that?" she repeated. "That horse was just scared! He needed a little patience!"

"Mary, I know that, and you know that, but that's not how everybody looks at it. They figure if they can force the horse to do what they want then they have the power, and the horse will give in to it. Makes 'em feel big and important. But then what you have is a battle of wills, rather than a co-operation between man and beast. And co-operation is so much nicer for everybody."

Mary looked at Willie silently, taking in what he said and feeling a new respect for the man whom she had always viewed as nothing more than a cowhand and friend — certainly not a horse expert. Her contemplation was suddenly interrupted by the announcer's voice calling out a familiar name over the loudspeaker.

"Our next rider is number thirty four, riding Lady White Cloud. You may enter the ring."

Mary and Willie were across the ring from the gate, but Mary was near enough to see the startled look that crossed Jody's face when she heard the name of her pony announced.

"Whoops, I forgot to tell Jody that I made up a show name for Lady!" she giggled. "But she's smiling now, so I guess she didn't mind too much."

Jody led Lady through the gate and jumped nimbly onto her bare back just as she had done countless times back at the stable. Lady White Cloud arched her neck proudly as Jody gathered up the reins and guided her to the first obstacle.

"Where's that girl's saddle?" Mary overheard someone ask as Lady walked smoothly over the bridge and trotted over the poles.

"I was wondering the same thing myself," came the reply. "I can't believe the judge is allowing it — but he must be, he's not saying anything to her."

Mary turned and opened her mouth in retort, but she shut it just as quickly when she felt Willie's strong grip on her arm.

"You just pay attention to what's goin' on in the ring," he said firmly.

Lady jumped easily over the bales and was now stepping gingerly across the sheet of plastic without missing a step.

"Go, Lady. You show 'em," Mary whispered to herself.

The barrels were next, and Lady negotiated them at a high-stepping trot, just as she did the old fence posts in the pasture field at home, never getting close enough to allow Jody's leg to touch them. And when Jody picked up the egg in the spoon, Lady walked as if on eggshells herself so as not to jiggle the spoon.

"Uh-oh, here comes the scary part," Mary

exclaimed as Jody placed the egg and spoon back on the barrel and walked to the umbrella hanging on the fence. Mary knew from the intense look of concentration on Jody's face that she was nervous about this too.

"Just pick it up slow and don't be nervous, or Lady will know it and be nervous too," Mary said to herself, hoping Jody would get her telepathic message.

It almost seemed as if she did get the message, so slowly did she pick up the gaily striped umbrella from the fence. Lady cocked her head and eyed the funny looking thing suspiciously, but she stood perfectly still, waiting for a signal from Jody to walk on. Jody instead held the handle of the umbrella in her left hand along with the reins and felt carefully with her right hand for the mechanism which would open it.

"It's OK, Lad," she said softly as Lady's ears cocked backward in their listening position. "Just gonna open the umbrella real easy," she continued, sliding her right hand

When she caught a glimpse of the striped material unfolding behind her head, Lady startled just slightly.

up ever so slowly, the umbrella beginning to come to life right behind Lady's ears.

"Too bad horses have such a wide range of vision. Lady wouldn't even be able to see that thing behind her otherwise," Willie commented.

"Shhhhh, Willie, I'm trying to pay attention," Mary said sternly.

"Well excuse me for livin'," Willie replied. "I'll be quiet from now on."

The umbrella was almost up. When she caught a glimpse of the striped material unfolding behind her head, Lady startled just slightly, cocking her head and sidestepping in surprise.

"Whoa, Lady," Mary and Jody said in unison. The umbrella was up, and Jody used her free hand to pat Lady's neck reassuringly. After the initial shock, Lady seemed to take the umbrella in stride as she had everything else Jody had ever carried on her back. Reassured by the calm tone of Jody's voice, she walked quietly on as Jody slowly lowered the umbrella and hung it back on the fence.

"Yes! That was the worst part!" Mary exclaimed a little too loudly, drawing looks from the pair who had spoken earlier about the absence of Lady's saddle. "Now she'll be perfectly fine!" she continued in their direction.

And Lady *was* just fine, accepting the jugs without a hitch and finishing the class by standing like a statue while Jody opened the gate with one hand, backed Lady through without ever letting go of the gate, and then fastened it behind them.

"Yay!!" Mary yelled, forgetting to be quiet and applauding loudly as Jody and Lady trotted away from the ring. And then, appreciative of the demonstration of sound horsemanship displayed by Jody in contrast to the previous rider, the crowd joined in and gave Jody and Lady a rousing round of applause.

6
Results

"JODY, THAT WAS SUPER!" Mary shouted, shaking Jody vigorously by the shoulders." Lady was the best!"

Jody giggled as Willie offered his own congratulations by shaking her hand. The trio stood by the pickup, feeding Lady a carrot and exclaiming over each obstacle in the course and how it had been expertly maneuvered.

"But, Mary, there's still more riders in the class. Somebody might do better."

"No way! But let's go back and watch. I want to see which obstacles the others spook at."

"Why, Mary Rose Morrow, I never thought I'd hear you say such a thing," Willie said sternly. "This horse show business is going to your head, and I want you to settle down right now and quit wishin' other people bad luck."

Mary looked at Willie in dismay and clamped her lips tight together, hanging her head in embarrassment.

"Well, I didn't really mean it that way. I just think Lady was the best, and I don't think anybody else is going to do as well, that's all. I didn't want to wish the others bad luck," she said apologetically. "Except maybe Janelle," she finished quietly so that only Jody could hear.

But Willie heard, and he had to turn away so that the girls couldn't see the smile that was spreading across his face in spite of himself.

"Well, anyway, you better git yourselves back over to the ring if you want to see the last of the others ride. Class'll be over soon," he said.

"Oh, Mary, you go. I can't watch the rest. I'm too nervous." Jody said, burying her face in Lady's mane.

"Nervous?" asked Willie. "What've you got to be nervous about now? You're all done your part."

"I know, but I just am. I just want to stay here with Lady and get ready for my next class."

"That's gonna be a while," Mary said, scanning the class list. "Next thing for you is the keyhole race, and there are four classes ahead of that."

"Well, why don't you hitch Lady to the truck, and we'll walk over and watch the last of the class. Then we'll be over there when they announce the ribbons," Willie suggested.

"Excellent idea, Willie! We want to be

there when Lady's blue ribbon is announced! And you're coming, too, Jode. You'll have to go up and accept your first place in person."

"Ooohh," was the only comment Jody could muster as she clung to Lady's mane.

"Come on, I'll tie her up. I'm the groom, don't forget, and I know how to do a perfect slip knot. There, she's snug as a bug..."

Mary was suddenly cut off by the voice over the loudspeaker. "This concludes Class number one, the obstacle course. We will announce the results of this class in just a few minutes. Our next class is class number two, the pairs class. All pairs please report to the gate."

Willie found himself standing alone at the truck, muttering "daggone girls" under his breath as Jody and Mary sprinted off in the direction of the prize booth after the first few words from the announcer's mouth. Then he hobbled off behind them to hear the results of the obstacle course. And although Willie would never admit it, he was almost as excited as they were.

"I have the results of Class number one, the obstacle course!" came loudly over the speaker. "Please report to the prize booth to collect your ribbon!"

Mary and Jody were already there, standing arm in arm and staring at the ribbons. There seemed to be hundreds of them, first through sixth place, fluttering on their cardboard holders and aching to be held and cherished by an ecstatic winner. Jody held her hand over her heart, for she felt that any second it would fly out of her chest as she awaited the announcement of the results.

"In sixth place, we have rider number twenty-three, Ashley Dann riding Sunny's Shadow."

"Well, at least I didn't get last place," Jody whispered as Ashley Dann, a small girl with freckles and red hair, happily took her green ribbon from the woman who had given Willie a hard time about the saddle and whose job had now progressed to giving out ribbons.

"Don't be silly, Jody," Mary said, but then shushed herself as the next announcement came.

"In fifth place, rider number twenty-eight, Mandy Turner on Surprise Package."

"Willie, I didn't get fifth or sixth place!" Jody whispered loudly as Willie arrived at the prize booth. Then she turned to Mary as a horrible thought occurred to her. "But, Mare, what if I didn't place at all? I might've gotten eighth place! They don't even give a ribbon for that!" she lamented as Mandy Turner collected her pink ribbon.

"Willie, will you keep her under control?" Mary said impatiently as she strained to hear the next announcement.

"Fourth place goes to rider number twelve, Eliza Stoner on Wizard of Oz."

Jody hid her face in her hands.

"And in third place, we have rider number twenty-nine, Allison Strong on Dynasty."

Mary smiled knowingly.

"Second place goes to Sara Martin on Lucky Shamrock."

"You got it, Jode. You got it, you got it," Mary said urgently, pulling Jody's hands from where they had flown over her ears as each announcement came.

"And in first place, winner of a blue ribbon for the obstacle course, is the horse and rider team of number thirty-four, Jody Stafford and Lady White Cloud!"

Jody imagined that the announcer said her name much more loudly than he had the others, and she was too stunned to notice Mary jumping up and down and Willie shaking her hand as the ribbon was handed to her.

"So we needed a saddle, did we?" Mary said smugly to no one in particular. Willie prodded her with his elbow to be quiet as the woman handed the ribbon to Jody.

Jody and Mary linked arms and cantered happily
toward the truck to tell Lady the astounding news.

"Thank you ma'am, appreciate that," Willie said to her, taking off his hat respectfully.

"My pleasure. Congratulations, young lady. I guess you did just fine without any old saddle, didn't you?" she said graciously.

Jody, clutching her ribbon to her chest, was too thrilled to reply. She and Mary linked arms and cantered happily toward the truck to tell Lady the astounding news of how together they had won a first place ribbon in the very first class of their very first horse show.

7
The Black Stallion

"Lady! Look what you won!" Jody yelled even before they reached the truck where they had tied her. "You got a first!" she continued, giving Lady all the credit, as though she had been riderless throughout the Obstacle Course.

As it turned out, it didn't matter what Jody said to Lady, because as the girls turned the corner of the truck to present her with her ribbon, they could only stop and stare. Where Lady had once been standing at the end of the lead rope, there was now nothing but empty space. Lady was gone!

Mary and Jody stood dumbfounded for an instant before Mary found her voice.

"Lad?" Mary said softly in disbelief. "Lady?" she called more loudly. Then, "Laaadyyy!" she yelled at the top of her voice, as both girls sprung into action, running around the truck, looking in all directions, even peering into the bed of the pickup, hoping Lady had somehow decided to jump in and go home on her own. But Lady was nowhere in sight.

"What's all the commotion?" Willie asked, limping back to the truck. "Where'd you put Lady?"

Willie!" Jody said in an absolute panic. "She's gone! She wasn't here when we got back and she's not anywhere around! You didn't move her, did you?"

"Me, move her? How could I move her when I was with you?" he asked. "Now, look, she must've broke loose from the lead rope.

92

See here, the snap's broke off," he said, holding up the end of the rope for the girls to see.

"She's probably just off visitin' with some other horses," he said, forcing his voice to stay calm for the sake of the panicky girls. "Now, settle down. There's nothin' to be done but to head off and look for her."

At that, the girls turned suddenly and ran smack into each other in their hurry to go off in all directions to look for Lady.

"Ow!" Mary yelped, rubbing the end of her nose where it had made a painful connection with Jody's shoulder.

"Sorry, Mare!" cried Jody helplessly, choking back a sob. "Oh, Willie, where should we look? Where do you think she could have gone?"

"First thing you got to do is calm down," Willie said, patting Jody awkwardly on the back. "We'll start by asking the people nearby here if they've seen her."

But their entreaties offered no clues, as the "people nearby" at their trailers had been watching the Obstacle Course and had seen nothing of a runaway pony.

"There's nothin' else to do but to split up and look for her," Willie instructed. "Now you two go over to the paddocks by the barn, and I'll look by the rings. Here, take a lead rope with you in case you find her."

"In case? But we will find her, Willie! Won't we?" cried Jody.

"Sure, you'll find her. I didn't mean that," Willie said reassuringly. "Now, go on."

The girls took off at a trot in the direction of the paddocks while Willie shuffled as quickly as he could go back to the rings. There the show continued, riders and horses unmindful of the potential tragedy unfolding nearby. Willie held his gnarled hand above his eyes, shading the sun as he squinted in all directions, hoping for even a glimpse of Lady's copper and white patches among the other horses. He almost hoped to hear the cry of "Heads up!" which signaled a loose horse running among the crowds. But no cry came, and Willie saw nothing. Then, as he was about to turn from the ring where Lady's next class was about to begin without her, he felt the grip of a hand like iron on his arm. He turned and looked down into Mary's distraught green eyes.

"We found her. We found her, Willie, and now we don't know what to do," she whispered anxiously. "You have to come." And with that, she turned and was off toward the paddocks, Willie going along behind her as fast as he could manage.

Willie and Mary were met halfway to the paddocks by a very disturbed and anxious Jody, hopping on either foot and biting her fingernails.

"Is she still in there?" Mary asked fearfully.

"What do you mean, is she still in there? Of course she's still in there. How do you suppose I could have gotten her out?"

"In where?" Willie asked impatiently. "And why haven't you got her out?"

"Oh, you'll see, Willie. You'll see. We're almost there."

As the three turned the corner of the barn, Willie stopped dead and stared, open-mouthed. There inside the paddock stood Lady, stretching her back and preening prettily while the black stallion, the gorgeous horse that Mary had noticed as they entered the show grounds, pranced and snorted and pawed in circles around her, his red nostrils flaring as he nickered and rubbed his muzzle on her beautifully arched neck.

"There she is, Willie," Mary said simply. "She's in there, and we can't get her out."

Willie said not a word. He shut his mouth and took off his hat so he could scratch the side of his head while he watched the coal-black stallion with a perfect white star on his forehead prance about the paddock. Finally Jody broke the silence.

"Willie, what should we do? We tried to

go in and get her, but he won't let us. He spins around and tries to kick, then he turns around again and tries to bite!"

"Well, he's just bein' a stallion, protecting his mare," Willie said wisely. "And what do you think you're doin', goin' in a paddock with a stallion like that? Ain't you got good sense?" he continued. Then Willie stepped up to the paddock fence and leaned over, admiring the black horse. "Look at that pretty star, right perfect between the eyes."

"Willie!" Mary demanded impatiently.

Willie shook himself out of his reverie and got back to the business at hand. "Now, I figure she musta seen him in there and decided she wanted to go in. See where that top board's broke off the fence? She either broke that off jumpin' in, or it was already broke, and she took the opportunity to use that low spot to get in."

The girls waited for him to go on, but Willie just stood watching Lady and the stallion rubbing noses. Finally, Mary could stand it no longer.

"Well, Willie, what are you going to do about it?" she fairly shouted. "We can't just leave her here! And aren't his owners going to get mad if they see Lady in there with their horse?"

"Just hold your horses," Willie replied. "We'll get her out. And everybody's too busy watchin' or takin' care of the show to come over here and see what's goin' on... I hope," he continued under his breath. As he spoke, Willie stared steadily at the stallion, trying to read his mind as he snorted and threw his splendid black head up and down. Then, without a word, hat in hand, Willie walked to the gate and began to unfasten the latch.

"Willie!" Jody yelled. "You can't go in there! He'll kill you!"

"Yeah, Willie!" Mary added. "Ain't you got good sense?"

"You just hush now, girl," Willie said to Jody. "And you keep Mary quiet too," he went on, opening the gate very slowly. The stallion cocked his head and eyed Willie wildly, snorting low through his flaring nostrils.

"How am I supposed to do that?" Jody began but stopped when Mary elbowed her in the ribs.

"Thanks a lot," Mary whispered, rather offended. "I *can* be quiet when it's important, you know."

Willie entered the paddock and stood just inside the gate only fifteen feet from Lady and the stallion. Lady nickered softly when she saw Willie and began to take a step toward him, but the stallion would have none of it. He stamped his foot and raised his head in challenge, snorting more fiercely this time. Willie made not a move but stood making a low, whirring sound in his throat, his hand outstretched. The stallion lowered his head and pawed the ground, raising small clouds of dust as he blew more softly through his nostrils, but he never took his eyes from Willie's.

"He's going to charge him!" Jody whispered, fighting back tears. "Mary, we can't let him stay in there!" And with that she took a step toward the paddock.

"Wait!" Mary answered, grabbing Jody's arm. "I think Willie knows what he's doing. I think he knows a lot more about horses than he's ever told us. Look at him now."

Willie had taken a few steps toward Lady and the stallion. He continued the low sound in his throat, alternating with soft words that the girls could not hear from where they stood. As Willie approached slowly, hand outstretched, the stallion raised his head with his ears pinned back and stomped once, stretching his head toward Willie and baring his teeth in challenge. But he never stepped forward or back, as though rooted to Lady's side. Willie continued forward, one careful step at a time, talking softly.

"He's getting close," Mary said. "Do you think the stallion's going to let him get close enough to get Lady?"

Before Jody could answer, the stallion decided he'd had enough of this intruder. With a mighty squeal and a shake of his head, he reared to his full height and lunged at Willie.

Mary and Jody screamed in unison, but their screams were drowned out by an even mightier sound from the paddock. As the stallion came down, a deep-throated roar such as the girls had never heard emitted from Willie's throat. He stood his ground and the stallion landed not more than a foot in front of him. The two were face to face, and the stallion actually looked stunned as he and Willie stared into each other's eyes. His ears were now up and he seemed more curious than evil.

"Now, settle down!" Willie growled, deep in his throat. "You settle down and behave yourself."

The stallion still did not move but snuffled and shook his head ever so slightly as Willie walked purposefully to Lady and put his hand on her halter. The stallion watched

With a mighty squeal and a shake of his head, he reared to his full height and lunged at Willie.

him closely and pawed the ground, but he never took a step forward as Willie led Lady firmly toward the gate. The girls gathered their wits about them enough to open the gate so that Willie could walk smoothly through with Lady. The stallion never budged until Lady was out and turned to nicker to him. Then, as if realizing he should act like a stallion, he ran to the fence, pinning his ears and baring his teeth as Willie led Lady away.

"Willie, how did you do that?" Mary and Jody jumped up and down around Willie as he led Lady back to the truck. "You scared him to death! He calmed right down when you told him to!"

Without a word, Willie tied Lady securely to the truck and began brushing her ruffled coat with a soft brush.

"Willie!" Mary insisted.

"That horse was just full of hisself for a minute, 'cause he had a mare with him," Willie finally replied. "He was well trained and he didn't mean no harm. Soon as somebody showed him who's boss, he knew it, and he settled down, that's all. Didn't take no magic to figure him out."

The girls silently began gathering up their brushes and supplies.

"Hey, you're signed up for a few more classes, ain't you?" Willie asked. "Why're you gettin' packed up now?"

"Willie, I think I've had enough horse show for one day," Jody replied wearily. "When Lady got loose, it scared me to death, and when the stallion almost killed you, it scared me even more. I guess I'm just worn out. And besides, I've got my one blue ribbon."

"Yeah, and next time maybe we'll even bring a dumb old saddle. Then nobody can complain, and we'll really show 'em!" said Mary confidently. "When we're done packing, I'll go scratch the rest of your classes, Jody. That's the groom's job!"

Willie shook his head and chuckled.

"Stallion almost killed me," he said under his breath and laughed out loud for the first time since Mary and Jody had known him. Then he finished brushing Lady and stood back for a good look at her. "Let's get Lady loaded up and go home," he said, patting her neck affectionately. "It'll be milkin' time before you know it."

8
Secret Place

"Jody, drop that broom! I'm in the mood for some adventure!"

Mary made this grand announcement from the loft in Lucky Foot Stable where she sat leafing through her dictionary as Jody swept the dirt floor clean of wayward pieces of straw.

"Listen to this: 'adventure: a journey on a road unknown!'" she quoted from the well-worn pages. "It's been yucky and rainy for so long, we've hardly been able to ride, and we haven't had an adventure since the horse show, and that's... (she counted on her fingers) almost four months ago!"

"Well, what should we do?" asked Jody. "It's a beautiful day today, and the ground is not so slippery. We could practice our circus act!"

"Noooo... I was thinking... it is a beautiful day, and we've mucked the stalls. I think... I think..." Mary paused dramatically at the sight of Jody's wide eyes and expectant face. "I think..." she said, whispering now, "we should ride to Secret Place."

"Oh, Mary, all the way there?" Jody murmured.

"Why not?" shouted Mary, swinging down from the loft by way of the rope swing. "It's June already, and it's warm and sunny and a good day for ridin'! Let's ask Gypsy and Ladabucks what they think!"

The girls burst through the stable door and ran out into the sunny pasture to find the ponies at the far end under the willow tree, drowsing nose to nose and lazily switching flies. They lifted their heads as one, pricking up their ears as the barefoot girls ran toward them with hair flying.

"Gypsy! Lady!" shouted Mary. "We're going to Secret Place!'"

"I thought we were going to ask them what they thought," giggled Jody.

"Of course they want to go. They love Secret Place!" And Mary wrapped her arms around Gypsy's neck in a great big hug while Jody kissed Lady gently on the nose.

Even before the barn swallows had finished feeding their young in the eaves of Lucky Foot Stable, the girls were ready to go. One side of each saddlebag was packed with the sandwiches they had each brought from home. Mary liked deviled ham, and Jody was especially fond of chicken salad. A fat cucumber was stuffed in Mary's bag and an apple in Jody's. Water bottles, always on hand in the stable, were filled with water from the hose and arranged carefully so as not to crush the sandwiches. The other side of the saddlebags were packed with the girl's favorite books of the moment — *The Secret Garden* for Jody and *Anne of Green Gables* for Mary.

Mary placed her saddlebags gently over Gypsy's withers and was just about to swing her leg over when Jody spoke up.

"Mare, do you think we should ride with our new saddles today and finish breaking them in?"

"No, today we're going bareback just like old times. See, the saddlebags are sitting just fine without a saddle! Time for a leg up! One, two, three!" and before Jody could say any more, she found herself on Lady's welcoming bare back and watched Mary swing up on Gypsy. They were off!

A ride to Secret Place was a rare thing because the round trip took from noon till sundown, and coming home through the woods and fields could be dark and scary.

"There's going to be a full moon tonight!" yelled Mary as they trotted down the long farm lane. "We'll travel home by the light of the silvery moon!" She began to sing, "By the light of the silvery moon! Whenever it's June, there's a silvery moon!"

"Mary, I don't think those words are exactly right," Jody giggled. Mary's mother had a collection of old records at home, and Mary liked to sing along with them, but she especially liked to make up her own words.

The girls rode the afternoon away through fields of summer wildflowers — trout lilies, star-of-Bethlehem, and stalks of mustard flower, some so tall they tickled the ponies' noses and made them sneeze. Late in the day, ahead in the distance they saw the first of the small forests on the way to Secret Place.

"The Piney Wood!" Mary yelled. "The dark and mysterious wood where footsteps make no sound and fairies whisper in the treetops! We shall enter here and partake of some refreshment!"

Just as Mary described, pine needles carpeted the ground of the wood and all was quiet and hushed. The smell was of Christmas, and the tops of the trees swayed together, filtering the sun and cooling the air inside. In the stillness, the ponies stepped slowly and carefully on the carpet of pine.

"Listen, Mary! The fairies!" whispered Jody reverently as the breeze murmured in the treetops.

"I hear them," Mary whispered back. Even Mary could be quiet in the Piney Wood. "Let's just stop for a minute and have a sip of water. We'll save the rest for Secret Place."

The next moments were spent sitting silently on the soft needles of the little forest, leaning against the rough bark of a tree, sipping water and breathing deeply of the cool, pine-scented air. Mary and Jody held the bridle reins loosely as the ponies snuffled curiously at the fallen pine cones. Finally, Mary began to grow impatient.

"Well, time's a-wastin'," she whispered. "Look, Gypsy's telling us to get moving!" The pony was doing just that, nuzzling

Mary's watch and nipping at her mop of brown curls. "Let's lead the ponies out of the pines and mount up in the open so we don't disturb the fairies."

"On to Secret Place, and quickly!" Mary shouted, once in the sunshine again. She bounced easily onto Gypsy's back and urged her into a jouncy trot.

"Mary, wait! I can't get on!" Jody called, running and hopping alongside Lady, who, deciding she wouldn't be left behind, had picked up a trot as well.

"Cease and desist!" Mary yelled, bringing Gypsy to a halt. "That means stop."

Mary and Gypsy waited patiently as Jody reined Lady in and hopped once, twice, three times, finally getting enough bounce to fling her leg over Lady's back and trot off down the path toward Secret Place.

Riding in silence and breathing the warm afternoon air, Jody watched as Mary raised her face to the sun and slowly leaned back, laying her head gently back on Gypsy's ample rump, her brown curls mixing with the pony's flaxen tail. Mary's head bobbed back and forth with the motion of the pony as Gypsy simply walked on as though there was nothing unusual about this style of riding. Jody relaxed by leaning forward onto Lady's neck, arms hanging comfortably down like a puppet, her blonde mane mixing with Lady's black one.

The girls rode along this way until the silence became too silent for Mary.

"'If I had a hammer'" she sang softly, "'I'd hammer in the morning'"... Then, "'I'D HAMMER IN THE EVENING,'" Mary sang at the top of her lungs, sitting up abruptly and suddenly urging Gypsy into a brisk trot.

"Look, Jody! Secret Place dead ahead! Heave ho! A-cantering we will go!" And off she and Gypsy flew with Lady and Jody close behind.

"Where's the Secret Entrance?" asked Jody, peering at the ground as they walked the ponies next to the thick underbrush bordering the trees surrounding Secret Place. The thicket looked impenetrable, but the girls had discovered the way in the year before. Once inside, it was like they had unearthed their own hidden realm. They never saw another soul there, and they had not shared the location with anyone. Now it was simply a matter of finding the almost invisible path.

"Quiet!" yelled Mary, "I'm looking for clues. The Diamond Rock is near here, I'm sure, and the Double-Trunked Tree. That's where the entrance is!"

"Mary, I think I see it! The Diamond Rock!" cried Jody.

"And the Double-Trunked Tree!" Mary added.

Sure enough, the huge old walnut tree loomed above, its trunk split and twisted by a long-ago lightning storm. At its base rested a craggy gray rock embedded with tiny bits of mica glittering in the late afternoon sun.

Next to the rock, invisible to all but an explorer's eyes, was a path scarcely a foot wide through the thicket.

"The Secret Entrance," Mary intoned reverently. "The sun is low. In we must go," she rhymed. Mary liked to rhyme almost as much as she liked to sing. Jody giggled as Mary led the way onto the Secret Path.

Deep inside the woods, daylight was shaded by the canopy of tall trees over the Path. Here, the horses stepped carefully, heads down, to avoid tripping on the gnarled tree roots criss-crossing the trail.

"Jody, look," Mary said suddenly, pointing at the ground, "it's the Forbidden Fork."

"Oh, I remember!" said Jody, looking down at the place in the Path where it split off in two directions. "What's the rhyme again?" she asked.

Mary placed her hand on her chest and chanted solemnly, "If you go to the left, you may meet with death; but a turn to the right, and you'll laugh with delight!"

Of course, the girls had never gone to the left, but they imagined all sorts of destruction awaiting them there. So, as always, they went to the right, continuing down the Secret Path toward the next destination.

"To the Roller Coaster Hill, and hurry!" Mary cried. "Daylight is waning! That means going away," she continued confidentially.

The ponies picked up a trot on the narrow path, and before long the girls came to the crest of a steep hill ending in a gully. They gazed silently down at the bottom of the hill for a moment before Mary grinned knowingly at Jody.

"Shall we?" asked Mary.

"Onward," declared Jody.

The ponies needed no encouragement. They had done this before! Pricking up their ears, they galloped wildly down the hill.

"And upward!" screamed Mary as the ponies jumped the gully in unison and raced madly up the other side. The girls reined them in at the summit and laughed with glee

Spreading below in rolling splendor was a beautiful valley dotted with pine trees and rhododendron bushes.

as Lady stamped and nipped at Gypsy's withers, and Gypsy squealed and snorted like the wild mare of Mary's imaginings. The Roller Coaster Hill was one of the most exciting parts of the trip to Secret Place.

"Let's walk the ponies and let them catch their breath," Mary suggested. "Then it's on to..." her voice trailed off.

"The... Haunted Mansion?" Jody whispered.

"Yep!" yelled Mary. "Let's go!"

The ponies didn't have far to go before reaching the furthest edge of the woods where the thick stands of trees gave way to a clearing. Emerging from the dim forest into the light, the girls stopped to catch their own breath at the sight that greeted them. Spreading below in rolling splendor was a beautiful valley dotted with pine trees and rhododendron bushes. Red and pink roses bloomed on sturdy bushes while purple iris and white peonies waved in the slight breeze from the woods. This had once been someone's hillside garden. Nestled in the prettiest part of the valley stood the burnt-out shell of an old stone house. The foundation and two sections of stone walls were the only parts of the house still standing.

"Hello, Haunted Mansion," Jody said with a shiver. A little way beyond the remains of the mansion, the slanted gray roof of a little red stable, undamaged by the fire, could just be seen through the trees. The stable had stood untouched for years with yellow straw, now dusty with age, still strewn about the three stalls inside. Behind the stable ran a wide stream of clear bubbling water. They had reached the heart of Secret Place, and the girls sighed with contentment at having arrived at last.

9
Misty's Barn

THE SLANTING RAYS of the setting sun lent an unearthly glow to the valley. It seemed to set the straw afire with a yellow blaze and made the "diamonds" glint in the rocks of the burbling creek as the water ran over them.

Mary and Jody would have stayed longer on the edge of the valley gazing at the splendor below, but Lady pawed the ground impatiently.

"Look," laughed Mary, "she wants to go see Misty's Barn."

The girls had decided on their first trip to Secret Place that Misty of Chincoteague had probably once lived in the little red stable.

"Lady, we'll get there, but our first stop, as always... Haunted Mansion!"

The ponies needed no urging to head down the hill into the valley below, as there was some very succulent grass awaiting them there. In no time they had almost reached the Mansion.

"Mary, do you think it's safe?" Jody asked. Jody knew the Haunted Mansion was safe, but she always asked Mary anyway.

"We'll soon see," Mary whispered mysteriously.

Creeping ivy climbed the stones of the remaining walls of the Mansion, and holes now gaped where windows had once been. It was to one of these openings that Jody rode Lady rather hesitantly, her heart beating a little faster than normal. Lady, however, always curious and not having any idea that the Mansion was haunted, immediately stuck her head and neck through the wide opening and sniffed expectantly.

Suddenly and without warning, Lady threw up her head, blew through her nostrils, reared up as high as she could, and spun around in a complete circle.

"Jody!" Mary shrieked, watching her friend grab frantically for mane as Lady reared straight up again. She was already hanging half off the pony's back from the previous spin, and Mary was sure Jody would fly off completely in the next instant, but miraculously she stayed on. Lady seemed to have forgotten she had a rider on her back, so wild did she become over what she saw in the Mansion. But just as suddenly as Lady began, she stopped dead and stood like a statue, her head up, nostrils still flaring, and eyes wide as she stared at the opening in the Mansion. Jody took this opportunity to straighten herself up and turn the mare's head away from the wall, and after much kicking and encouragement, away from the Mansion altogether.

"Jody!" Mary shrieked, watching her friend grab
frantically for mane as Lady reared straight up again.

"Jode, are you alright?" Mary asked, shaking almost as hard as Jody.

"I think I need to get off for a minute," Jody answered, sliding down from Lady's back. "What do you think she saw?"

"Here, you hold Gypsy and I'll investigate," Mary said bravely. Jody was only too glad to stand away from the Mansion holding the two ponies.

"Mary, be careful. Maybe it really is haunted. Horses can sense these things, you know."

"Nonsense! If there's a ghost in there I'll chase him out!" Mary said, not feeling nearly as courageous as she sounded.

Mary picked her way through a tangle of vines growing at the base of the Mansion until she reached the opening. Then, standing on her tiptoes, she peered in.

"Aaaahhh!" Mary shrieked. She turned to run back to Jody but got her feet tangled up in the vines and fell flat on her face.

"What is it!? What is it!? Mary!" Jody

yelled, not able to go to Mary's aid because of the pony she held in each hand.

"Ahhh...Ahhh...Haaheeehaaahaa," Mary laughed, face down in the tangled ivy. She rolled over on her back and laughed uncontrollably, holding her stomach and trying to catch her breath.

"Mary!! What? Will you tell me what is so funny? What's in there?"

"Oh...Oh, sorry, Jode, I'm laughing because it's just a stupid old black snake sunnin' itself on the ledge inside the window. But when it lifted up its head to check me out it scared me to death! Must've scared Lady too. But it's not scared the least bit!"

Jody shivered at the thought of the "stupid old black snake" because she really wasn't too fond of snakes and was glad she hadn't seen it herself. But she didn't let Mary know that.

"Oh, is that all?" she commented nonchalantly. "Lady, I'm surprised at you. It's just a stupid old snake."

"Go look for yourself," Mary invited, still chuckling.

"Oh, no," Jody said quickly. "I mean, I think we should go down to the stable now. Lady needs to calm down, and she loves Misty's barn."

"True enough!" shouted Mary, scampering up from her nest in the ivy. "Let's go!"

When the girls reached the open dutch door of the little red stable, they could see it looked the same as they remembered. Cobwebs adorned every corner and dust lay thick on the slanted stone windowsills. The windows were still intact but so covered with dirt that they couldn't be seen through. Black rubber water buckets, crisscrossed over the openings with spiderwebs, still hung in the stalls, and the wooden mangers still held a few dried up corncobs. The stable was indeed tiny with three small stalls and barely enough room for a pony to walk down the aisle.

"Look!" cried Jody, peering through the

dim light of the doorway. "Look at those saddle racks back in the corner! I never noticed them before!"

"Me either!" said Mary. She led Gypsy straight through the door, down the aisle past the stalls, and into the back corner of the stable.

"Look at this! They have names on them! Little brass plates with the horse's names!" Mary said excitedly.

Of course, the saddles that had rested on the racks were long gone, but sure enough, the three wooden racks that remained each had a small brass nameplate still attached. Jody stood in the doorway with Lady as Mary dusted off the nameplates in the gathering twilight.

"Let's see... I can hardly make it out... this one says... Eclipse!" Mary said. "That's a neat name — he must've been born during the total eclipse of the moon! And... Kiss & Tell?! I wonder where that one came from? And, last but not least..." Mary stopped.

She didn't say anything for a long time.

Finally Jody said, "Mary, what is it? Can you read it? Mary?"

"Oh, Jode," Mary whispered.

"What? What is it?" Jody insisted, wishing there was enough room for her and Lady to join Mary and Gypsy in the corner.

"Jody, you won't believe it." Mary said dramatically. "You know what it says?"

"No, WHAT!?" exclaimed Jody, getting more than a little impatient.

"It says... It says... Misty," Mary said, eyes wide with amazement.

"Does it really?" Jody said in awe.

Mary nodded as the two girls shivered deliciously. Lady, however, not sensing the gravity of the moment, nickered anxiously for Gypsy to join her outside the stable.

"I have an idea," Jody said. "Come on out, Mare, and let's sit by the creek and eat while we let Gypsy and Lady go wading. Then we should start heading home."

"Jolly good! I'm starved!" yelled Mary,

her hunger pangs overcoming the mysterious matter of Misty.

10
Runaway Ponies

THE GIRLS LED LADY and Gypsy to the very edge of the creek and tied a knot in their reins, so they wouldn't drag in the water. The ponies lowered their heads and snuffled the rippling stream as it rushed over smooth pebbles. Gypsy took a step in and pawed once, then buried her nose deep in the water.

"That shows a horse with real spirit!" laughed Mary.

But Lady was not to be outdone. Wading boldly out to the middle of the creek where the water was knee deep, she pawed a few times, then dropped to her knees, laid down, and tried to roll!

"Lady!" shrieked Jody. "That water's cold!"

And as Lady went down on her side, she seemed to agree, for just as quickly as she went down, she scrambled up again, leaving Jody with a half-wet, half-dry pony.

"She's gonna be fun to ride home!" giggled Mary. "Look, Gypsy's decided to be nice and stay on her feet." Sure enough, Gypsy stood next to Lady, watching curiously as Lady shook herself like a wet dog. She pawed gingerly at the water, not about to try anything new.

"We should let them stay in and have fun while we eat," Jody suggested, but Mary had already flung open her saddlebag and was unwrapping her deviled ham sandwich. Jody sat down and carefully took her chicken salad from its wrapper, all the while keeping an eye on the wading ponies. Gypsy and Lady pawed and splashed happily in the stream, snorting through their noses, switching their wet tails and flinging creek water every which way.

"Hey!" Jody complained as the water hit her sandwich.

"Getting too dark to read," Mary said, wistfully flipping through the pages of *Anne of Green Gables*. "We'd better head back soon — by the light of the silvery moon!"

Just at that moment, Gypsy and Lady suddenly stopped their splashing, flung up their heads, and stood as still as statues, peering into the woods. An instant later, the ponies snorted like wild things, whites showing in their eyes and nostrils flaring red.

"What is it?" whispered Jody.

Mary pointed upward. "Look! At the top of the hill!"

At the edge of the valley where the girls had stood not so long before, in the dim light the girls saw not one, not two, but a whole family of deer — four in all. The majestic buck held his head high, showing off

Gypsy and Lady stood as still as the family of deer as they stared at each other for another instant.

his perfect rack of antlers, while his doe and two fawns stared down at the ponies in the creek.

"Where did they come from?" Mary whispered. "Wow, look at that buck. I don't think the buck is usually with the doe in the summer. I read a book about it. We're lucky to see all of them at once!"

"Look at the ponies," Jody murmured.

Gypsy and Lady stood as still as the family of deer as they stared at each other for another instant. Then, through some wild and unknown signal that only animals understand, the deer turned on their heels and were gone. As if one with the deer, the ponies spun around, leapt from the creek, and took off galloping as fast as they could go up the Roller Coaster Hill!

Jody and Mary were so stunned by this turn of events that they simply sat, mouths open, staring after the fleeing ponies. Of course, it was Mary who found her voice first.

"To the rescue!" she shrieked, jumping up and scattering food everywhere.

"Oh, Mary, where do you suppose they went?" lamented Jody, wringing her hands anxiously. "And how are we ever going to catch them?"

"Onward and upward," Mary said, pointing up the hill, and the girls took off at a gallop themselves after the runaway ponies.

The swiftly falling darkness proved quite an obstacle for the girls in their search for the wayward ponies as they crested the hill and started off through the woods.

"Now, what would the Indians do?" Mary wondered aloud. "They'd look for clues along the forest floor," she answered herself.

"And the tree branches," added Jody.

"What?" Mary said, a little annoyed with Jody for breaking her train of thought.

"The tree branches," Jody insisted. "They'd see if any were broken or bent."

"I guess you're right," agreed Mary. "I've got it. You look for broken branches, and I'll look on the ground for hoofprints and stuff."

Without another word, the girls turned and walked off in opposite directions, then they turned again and looked at each other in dismay.

"Mary! We have to stay together. Don't we?"

"Of course! Of course we do!" said Mary. "But I don't know which way we should start off."

"Oh, suppose they've gone out and crossed the road! And it's almost dark now," Jody lamented, feeling as though she would cry very soon.

"Now, don't start that, Jody. We have to be brave, and... and... keep our wits about us! I read that in a book once. You're right, though. The ponies would probably head out the same way we came in. So let's follow the Secret Path, and everwho sees a clue first, holler!"

And so they set off, Mary with her eyes glued to the ground and Jody staring up at any tree branch that might possibly have been altered by the ponies galloping by. The nightly chorus of tree frogs began in earnest as the girls walked along the Secret Path in silence, and in the distance, a lonely owl called to its mate.

Suddenly, Mary stopped and put a finger to her lips.

"Listen!" she whispered. "Did you hear something?"

"Just the owls," Jody said.

"No, no, I could have sworn I heard the sound of hooves walking on the path."

The girls strained their eyes ahead on the path but saw nothing.

"I don't hear it anymore. Let's keep going," Mary said.

"Mary, maybe if we called and whistled they would come," Jody suggested.

"Hmmm, maybe. It's worth a try! You go first," Mary said generously.

Jody pursed her lips and blew her special whistle — one long note and two short — that she always used to call Lady in from the pasture at home.

"Laaaady! Ladabucks!" she called, then stopped and listened.

They heard nothing.

"Let me try," said Mary.

Putting a finger in each corner of her mouth, she blew one long shrill whistle followed by four short melodious notes. The girls listened intently but still heard not a sound. By now it was nearly dark in the woods, the light of the full moon almost obliterated by the thick canopy of leaves. Mary and Jody clutched each other's hands, walking carefully down the Secret Path where they had ridden happily a short while before.

Again, Mary stopped and listened.

"I heard it that time!" Jody exclaimed. "I did hear a noise — like shuffling or something!"

"Me too!" Mary said. The girls peered around once more.

Silence.

Walk a few steps.

"I only hear it when we're walking!" Mary whispered.

So they walked on. Before they had taken another ten steps, the shuffling noise could be heard again over the noise of the tree frogs.

"It's behind us!" Jody said.

The girls turned slowly around to face the blackness behind. And then, as they stood squinting into the dark, the light of the moon shone through the drifting clouds to reveal the ghostly forms of the two wayward ponies, standing directly behind the two miserable, frightened girls!

"GYPSY!" screamed Mary, flinging her arms wildly around the wide-eyed pony's neck.

"Oh, Lady," sighed Jody, stroking the pony's nose as she fought back tears of relief.

"Don't ever do that again! You must have been so scared!"

Lady nickered softly and lipped at Jody's straight blonde hair. Then Jody heard another sound nearby — soft and low — the familiar sound of Mary's giggle. It began quietly, like a brook bubbling up from the ground, then exploded into full blown laughter.

"They were right behind us the whole time!" Mary laughed. "They followed us down the Secret Path! And we were so worried!"

Jody giggled happily with Mary and gave Lady a great big pony hug. Gypsy rubbed her head up and down, up and down on Mary's arm while Mary composed herself enough to begin giving orders.

"OK, troops!" she commanded, "about face, mount up, homeward bound! It's getting late! Everwho is the last one out of Secret Place is a rotten egg!"

Mary gave Jody a quick leg up and then jumped nimbly onto Gypsy's back.

"By the light of the silvery moon... whenever it's June, there's a silvery moon!" Mary sang gaily as the two girls headed down the Secret Path and out of the woods, trotting merrily home in the moonlight.

11

Panic in the Pasture

THE UNUSUALLY HOT summer that commenced after the trip to Secret Place prevented the girls from riding as much as they wanted to, but as cooler fall weather approached, they were ready for some excitement on horseback. A refreshing crispness in the air replaced the stifling humidity of August, and the ponies responded to the change in weather by kicking up their heels like stallions when they were turned out to pasture. Even the cows seemed more lively in the brisk morning air, sometimes even picking up a trot on their way in for milking.

Mary and Jody loved this time of year more than any other — the geese honking overhead as they made their way to their winter homes, leaves cascading from the trees in a riot of color, and the funny shapes and sizes of the pumpkins dotting Mr. McMurray's field.

"Let's practice our circus act in the pasture," Mary suggested one cool and breezy Saturday morning. The girls led the ponies from Lucky Foot Stable into the field, but even before they had a chance to shut the gate, Lady and Gypsy began dancing and snorting in a most unusual manner. The girls knew that even the autumn air wasn't enough to get them this excited.

"Whoa, Gypsy! Calm down, for pete's sake," Mary admonished the nervous mare. "What in the world is wrong with you?"

"Mary, do you hear something?" Jody asked, tilting her head quizzically to one side, holding firmly to Lady's reins.

"I was just about to ask you the same question," Mary replied. "What is that noise?"

A crackling sound like very loud static from a radio was coming from somewhere above. The girls looked skyward at the thick black electric wires strung between the tall brown telephone poles that lined the road next to the pasture.

"What in the..."

Before Mary could finish her sentence, one of the thick black wires snapped, and cracking like a whip, it sizzled and fell, writhing like a snake along the ground. The ponies spooked and jerked the reins from the girls' hands, reared up, and galloped as fast as they could back to the stable!

Mary and Jody, too astounded to move or run after the galloping ponies, watched in horror as the electric line snaked along the ground as if alive, heading directly for a group of cows standing placidly in the pasture. Cows are not nearly so nervous as horses, and they will usually not run off at the first sign of trouble. And Mary and Jody both knew this was serious trouble.

"Cows! Come along! Into the barn!" Mary shouted with all her might.

"Hrup! Hrup!" Jody added, using the call she had heard Willie use. But it was no use. The cows just stood there as, suddenly, the sizzling end of the black wire snapped into the air with a loud crack like a bullwhip. As Mary and Jody watched helplessly, the terrible wire came down directly on the back of a poor unsuspecting cow at the edge of the group, knocking her instantly to the ground before snaking away. It finally came to rest away from the cows, sizzling and quivering but still, as if its power had been spent.

"Mary!" Jody screamed, starting toward the fallen cow. Mary reached out and grabbed her arm, squeezing it tight.

"Jody, don't you go one step further," Mary said sternly. "You stay away from that cow and that wire. We have to get Willie."

Jody did as she was told, but she couldn't

take her eyes off the fallen cow. Mary fairly dragged her away from the awful scene to the cow stable, where she knew Willie would be scooping feed into the troughs, preparing for the afternoon milking.

"What in the world?!" Willie exclaimed, as the girls burst through the door into the cow stable.

"Willie! You've got to come on the double!" Mary cried. "The electric wire broke and fell on one of the cows, and I think she's hurt real bad!" In her great excitement, Mary forgot to be careful of her grammar.

Willie's face turned as pale as the whitewashed walls of the cow stable.

"Whereabouts?" he asked shakily.

"Right in the far corner of the cow pasture by the old weeping willow tree!" Jody exclaimed.

Without another word, Willie hobbled out the door as fast as his old legs could carry him, the girls close behind.

"She's right over there..." Mary began,

During the time it had taken for the girls to fetch Willie, a cow ritual had taken place.

pointing to the far corner of the pasture where the poor cow had collapsed. But the strange sight that greeted them there stopped them in their tracks. The cow could no longer be seen, having been completely surrounded in a perfect circle, by the group of twenty other cows in the pasture. Their heads were in, hindquarters out. During the time it had taken for the girls to fetch Willie from the dairy barn, a cow ritual had taken place.

"Well, I ain't never..." Willie began.

"What do you think they're doing?" whispered Jody.

"Why, they're... they're having a funeral, of course," Mary said matter-of-factly. "They're gathering around the cow to pay their respects."

"Well, payin' their respects or not, they're too close to that electric line," Willie said. "I got to chase them away from there."

"We'll help you, Willie. Jody, get some sticks," Mary said, already halfway to the willow tree.

"No, you won't neither," Willie said stern-ly. "You'll just keep yourselves away from that wire and that cow, you hear?"

Mary and Jody had never seen Willie quite so agitated. A flush crept across his weather-beaten face, and the tone in his voice told them he expected to be obeyed. Mary stopped in her tracks as Willie strode past her to the weeping willow, where he broke off a long branch and brandished it resolutely in the air.

"Hey up! Hey up!" Willie yelled, swinging the branch wildly as he approached the herd of cows encircling their friend. "Git away from there! Git away, I say!"

A few of the cows turned their heads to look at Willie dumbly, but not one of them budged an inch from their chosen position. This unexpected disobedience prompted Willie to swing his branch even more furi-ously, even whacking a couple of the cows across the rump.

"Git up, I say. In the barn — it's milkin' time!" Willie tried, although it wasn't milking time at all, and unfortunately the cows knew it. A few shifted uneasily in their places, but none would turn away to head for the barn, choosing instead to remain steadfastly staring at their fallen companion.

"Mary," whispered Jody, an unwelcome lump forming in her throat, "do you think she's dead?"

Mary thought silently for a moment before turning to Jody.

"Well, the way I figure it, there was an awful lot of electricity in that wire. It hit the cow right on the back, and the cow hasn't moved. I think... I think... she's probably not gonna get up again."

With that, she turned and busied herself watching Willie, but Jody could see the glint of a tear in the corner of Mary's eye.

12
The Cow
Funeral

WILLIE SOON GAVE up the idea of having the cows leave their place in the circle. Knowing the habits of cows as well as he did, he decided to try another way. Laying down his stick, he walked determinedly across the pasture to the big sliding door of the cow stable and turned to face the group of cows. Then he did something he had done every morning and afternoon for the past forty years: he called the cows in for milking.

"Hrup! Hrup! Come on! Come on! Come

on! Hrup! Hrup!" Willie called deeply, his worn and weathered hands cupped around his mouth. "Come on!"

Again, the cows knew it wasn't milking time yet. But, being creatures of habit, the old familiar call began to take effect.

"Look, Mare, they're listening," Jody murmured.

Several of the cows turned their heads in the direction of the barn. As if struggling with a decision, they stomped the ground and shook their heads, snorting and letting out short bawls of frustration like calves when they're first being weaned from their mothers.

"Hrup! COME ON!" Willie continued, a note of desperation creeping into his voice.

"Willie's going to give up soon," Mary said. "I don't know what he's going to do if this doesn't work."

And then, the cows seemed to make their decision. Turning suddenly as if all of one mind, they headed for the barn as they had done hundreds of times before. But this time, rather than the slow, methodical walk of a cow going in for milking, they trotted, cantered, and some even galloped, kicking up their heels like frisky calves. It seemed once they had made up their minds to leave their friend, they couldn't get away quickly enough.

"Look at them, Mary! They're running! Have you ever seen anything like it before in your life?"

"Nope, and neither has Willie!" Mary giggled.

Sure enough, Willie's mouth hung wide open as the cows descended upon him in their hurry to get to the barnyard. Mary and Jody laughed when Willie had to actually jump out of the way of the stampede.

Believing everything was fine then, they turned once more to look at the poor felled cow.

"Oh, no!" they shouted in unison.

The reason for their dismay stood rooted

to her spot in the pasture like a statue. While all the other cows settled comfortably in the barnyard, waiting for Willie to let them in the stable for milking, one stubborn cow remained steadfastly by the side of her fallen friend.

"Mary, what is she doing?" Jody asked, glancing nervously at the barn in anticipation of Willie storming out with another willow branch.

"Why, it's her best friend, of course," Mary explained. "She won't leave her, and she shouldn't. I certainly wouldn't leave you if you were in the same predicament."

"And I wouldn't leave you, either," Jody responded quickly. "Oh, but Mary! Here comes Willie! What's he going to do now?

Willie strode across the pasture toward the two cows, picking up the willow branch on his way.

"Well, he won't understand about the best friend business," Mary said. "A cow's just a cow to him, and his job is to keep them safe."

"NUMBER 29!" Willie shouted. "COME ON!" Willie knew all the cows by the plastic number tags that hung around their necks.

"Daggone stubborn wench!" he said under his breath, just loud enough that Mary and Jody heard.

"Willie's really mad," Mary giggled. "Did you hear that?"

"Mary, it's not funny! He's going to hit the poor thing, when all she's doing is being loyal to her friend!"

Sure enough, Willie brought the branch up and swung it hard across the cow's broad back. The branch wasn't very thick and so green and soft that it just sort of bent when it came down, having no effect whatsoever on the cow. This made Willie madder still.

"Git up! Git up, I say!" Willie yelled, waving the bent green switch above his head. But Willie may as well have been a bothersome old fly, for as much attention as the cow was paying him. Never turning her head

"*Well, daggonit, go ahead and stand there and get electrocuted then!*" *Willie said finally.*

even to look Willie's way, she continued to stand and stare at her poor friend.

"Well, daggonit, go ahead and stand there and get electrocuted then!" Willie said finally.

Throwing down his switch in disgust, he turned and limped back to the barn to tend to the other cows.

"What do we do now, Mare?" Jody asked.

Before Mary could answer, the cow suddenly turned her head and looked straight at the two girls. Then she raised her head, stomped her foot, snorted just once, turned around, and ran to the barn. Mary and Jody were dumbfounded.

"Have you ever seen a cow run that fast?" Jody asked.

"Today was the first time I've ever seen cows run, period!" Mary replied. "Walk, usually, trot occasionally, but never run! She must have just noticed everybody else left! Look, there she goes straight into the barnyard. Won't Willie have a fit when he sees her?"

"We'd better go see about the ponies,

Mare — I think the excitement's over for one day," Jody said, walking toward the pasture gate.

The girls had barely turned around to head back to Lucky Foot Stable when yet another astonishing sight stopped them. Emerging from the open door of the barnyard came Number 29, walking with a slow dignity that was in sharp contrast to the wild gallop she had displayed just minutes before. And behind her, in a perfectly straight line of black and white, came the rest of the herd. Had they turned their heads to look, they would have seen Mary and Jody standing stock-still, their mouths open wide in surprise, as the strange procession passed. But they looked neither right or left but walked on as one. Poor Willie stood in the doorway of the stable, watching them go, and sighing in resignation as he threw his hat down in dismay.

"Mary, what are they going to do now?" Jody whispered.

"Well, as far as I can tell, Number 29 was upset that everybody sort of ran off like they did without taking time to pay their last respects. So she went back to get them. I guess when she thinks they've spent enough time, she'll give them a signal."

"Do you really think cows are that smart?" Jody asked.

"Well, I never did, but something is going on in their brains! Let's just wait and see."

By this time, the cows had arranged themselves in the same circle as before. They stood quietly, heads down, as if in prayer. Mary and Jody heard a rustle in the grass and turned, surprised to see Willie with his hat in his hands.

"Daggone cows," he murmured, trying without success to sound grumpy. There was a new respect in his voice for the creatures he thought he knew so well. "It's milkin' time in five minutes," he continued. "We'll see if they remember."

The three stood silently, bowing their heads along with the cows. The chirping of birds was now the only sound in the quiet pasture. It seemed as if they had stood there for an eternity when suddenly, Number 29 raised her head. She backed slowly from the circle and turned away from the group, walking toward the barn. The others never moved. Only when she was halfway to the cow stable did she stop and turn back. Then, stretching her neck and opening her mouth in a perfect *o*, she called the other cows just as a mother cow calls her calf — a sound that is very hard to describe if you have never heard it. Much higher pitched than a regular moo, the call is repeated over and over in rapid succession.

"Well, I'll be..." Willie said under his breath as the herd of cows responded by turning quietly away from their spots in the circle, lining themselves up once again in a perfectly straight black and white procession and walking to the barn as though nothing unusual had happened, and just as they had done every day of their lives at milking time.

The girls watched silently as the cows walked straight into the barnyard, and smiled when Willie, his hat still off in respect, followed them in.

"I think even Willie learned something about cows today," Jody commented.

"I know I did," Mary replied. "I never would have believed it if I hadn't seen it with my own eyes."

"I know," Jody said quietly. "But I think that cows probably have the same feelings we do, only they can't put them into words. Their feelings come from someplace they don't even understand, and when something like this happens, they just kind of feel what to do."

Jody looked at Mary to see if she was listening, but Mary was staring strangely at the spot above where the electric wire had snapped.

"Mare? What's wrong?" Jody asked. There was no reply.

"Mary, what is it?" Jody asked again.

"I was just thinking..." Mary said slowly. "What if... what if..."

"What?" Jody insisted.

"Well, the ponies are out here every day, and we're out here half the time sitting under the willow tree watching them graze, and we were just about to come out here and practice our circus act..." Mary pointed to where the cow still lay. "What if..."

"Mary, don't think about that," Jody said firmly. "Come on... We've got to check on Lady and Gypsy and tell them about the cow's funeral. No telling what mischief they've gotten into back at the stable. Willie's probably called the electric company by now, and they'll come and fix the wire."

Mary nodded solemnly, and without another word, the girls started off for Lucky Foot Stable to tend to the ponies.

13
The Tree

MARY AND JODY were excited. Christmas was only a week away! The first snow of the season had begun to fall that morning, by afternoon covering the ground and hiding the clumps of straw in the paddock just outside Lucky Foot Stable. The girls bustled around inside, sweeping and tidying up, their breath making little clouds in the chilly air, while Colonel Sanders watched from his perch on the top board of Lady's stall.

Lady stood looking out of her window

and nickered as if calling to the snow while Gypsy stomped her foot impatiently.

"Look, Mary, they want to go out and taste the snow," Jody giggled. "Let's turn them out in the big pasture and see what they do."

"OK, then we can clean their stalls and figure out what we're going to do today," Mary replied energetically, raising a cloud of dust as she swept in her usual vigorous manner. She threw down her broom and skipped to Gypsy's stall, fastening a lead rope to her halter.

When Jody and Mary led the ponies outside, the first thing they did was lower their muzzles to the snow. Gypsy lipped at the cold stuff cautiously, while Lady buried her nose in it, well past her nostrils and pushed a furrow before her as she walked, blowing out to keep the snow from going in. Mary and Jody laughed and skipped along, kicking snow in the air as they made their way to the pasture.

The instant the girls unclipped the lead

ropes from their halters, Gypsy and Lady were off across the pasture, kicking up their heels and throwing their heads up in the frosty air. Snow was still falling softly, making little white puffs that stuck to the girls' hair and eyelashes like tiny pieces of confetti. Mary flung out her arms and spun around in circles, sticking out her tongue to catch the snowflakes while Jody giggled at her silliness.

"Let's make angels," Jody suggested suddenly, and before she could say another word, Mary fell backward in the snow, arms still outstretched and flapping crazily up and down to make angel wings. Jody followed suit and the two lay in the snow, laughing and flapping their "wings" and catching snowflakes while the ponies snorted and pawed and sniffed them, Gypsy lipping Mary's brown curls and Lady pushing snow onto Jody with her muzzle. The girls abruptly jumped up, and the ponies took off in mock fright at a canter across the pasture.

"Look, they're going to roll!" Jody cried gleefully. Normally, rolling ponies were a cause for dismay, as they loved to roll in the dirt or mud just after a good grooming, but today the snow would only make their winter coats gleam.

"Look at Lady, Jode. She's gotten so fat she can barely roll over!" Mary laughed.

"That's not true!" Jody retorted indignantly.

But it was true, and Jody had to admit it to herself as she watched Lady struggle to turn over even once in comparison to Gypsy's four times.

"You know what they say, Jody. Every time a horse rolls over, he's worth a hundred dollars. Looks like Gypsy's worth at least four... no, there she goes again... five hundred dollars!"

Jody didn't reply as she watched Lady pull herself up heavily from the ground after only rolling once, and that had required great effort.

"That's an old wive's tale, Mary, and you know it!" Jody said, crouching down to grab a handful of snow.

"And Lady's starting to look like an old wife!" Mary replied with a wicked smile. Jody needed no more incentive to chase Mary out of the pasture. The snowball she had formed landed neatly on the back of Mary's head as she ran through the gate with a laugh.

"Wait a minute, Jode. We shouldn't have turned the ponies out! We could get our tree today!" Mary suggested, fluffing her hair to get the snow out. "Christmas will be here before we know it!"

"It is a perfect day for it!" Jody agreed. "And if we get it now, we'll have plenty of time to trim it!"

So back into the pasture they ran, catching the ponies and trotting them back to the stable. There they bridled them up and gathered the necessary supplies. The saddlebags were put to good use carrying the limb saw and a length of rope needed to bring the tree home. They each made sure to pack a stout pair of gloves to protect their hands from the cold and from the prickly tree trunk. Finally, a handful of horse treats were added to the bags to help sustain the ponies on the trip home.

"Ready!" Mary shouted as she leapt onto Gypsy's back, kicking up a dusting of powdery snow. Jody led Lady to an old tree stump to mount up, because, although Jody would never admit it, Lady really had gotten terribly fat over the summer and fall, and it was getting harder to mount bareback over her round belly.

As the foursome turned to head down the long farm lane, Finnegan came bounding from around the barn, tossing up snow with his muzzle, and yelping in excitement as he sensed the impending adventure with the girls.

"Tally ho! And off we go!" Mary laughed, watching Finnegan roll over and over in the snow at the pony's feet. "Come on, Finney!"

Jody got in line behind Mary and Gypsy, Finnegan ambling closely behind as they picked up a trot down the lane. Their destination was a field of pine trees at the far end of the farm that could not really be called a "piney wood" like the one at Secret Place because of its sparse population of trees. But the girls liked it because it possessed all sorts of natural decorations that could be put on the tree once it was set up in the stable.

Mary kept up a lively pace, singing *Jingle Bells* at the top of her voice while Jody brought up the rear, kicking Lady to try and keep up. But Lady would have none of it, taking her good old time and nipping Jody on her booted foot when she felt she had been nudged a bit too hard.

"Come on, Jode! Keep up! We're almost there!" Mary urged. At the next bend, she turned Gypsy off the snowy trail and into the field where the pine trees grew here and there along with holly bushes full of shiny red berries; rose hips; and tall, reedy plants with bushy tops turned brown and yellow from the frost. Mary liked to call them "bulrushes" for lack of their correct name. All these were lightly dusted with snow and would make perfect natural decorations for the tree.

"Jody! Will you come on?" Mary yelled, already trotting Gypsy around one tree and then another, scrutinizing each with a practiced eye. "I need you to help me pick one out!"

"We're coming; we're coming!" Jody shouted in exasperation, finally guiding Lady from the trail into the field of pines.

"Thanks for staying with us, Finney," she whispered to Finnegan, who had slowed his pace to match that of Lady.

"There you are!" Mary called impatiently. "It's about time!"

The evergreens that dotted the snow-covered field were of various heights and shapes and types, some tall with sparse and thinning branches, others short and bushy. Jody and Lady had no sooner set foot in the field than Mary yelled, "Here it is! I've found it!"

"I thought you needed my help," Jody said wryly.

"Well, come and look at this!" Mary said proudly. "You'll have to agree!"

Jody trotted Lady to where Mary sat on Gypsy. She looked in all directions, up at the trees surrounding them, and finally at Mary.

"Where?" she asked.

"Where? Right there!" Mary replied, pointing at the tree directly in front of them.

Jody looked up at the tree and then at Mary in disbelief.

"Mary, that tree is huge! We could never get it home with the ponies. I was hoping you meant that little tree right over there. It's so cute!"

"Jody! That dinky little thing? It barely has any branches!" Mary laughed. "All the decorations in the world wouldn't improve that one!"

"Well, at least we could get it home! How

are you going to transport yours, by train?" Jody retorted, crestfallen at Mary's criticism of her tree.

"Not at all!" Mary replied. "Look at the top of the tree! It's perfect!"

Jody looked up at the spot where Mary pointed, and then at Mary, who grinned with delight at the fresh challenge. As Mary's idea slowly sunk in, Jody began to shake her head, slowly at first, then all the more vigorously as Mary nodded happily.

"Oh, no. Oh, no," she said. "Mary Rose Morrow, you are not going up that tree. Over my dead body will you go up that tree!"

"Oh, Jody, settle down. We climb the horse chestnut tree at the barn all the time, and it's taller than that!"

"Yes, but we're not trying to cut the top out of it, either!" Jody protested. "You're going to get killed!"'

As though following the conversation, Finnegan sat at the ponies' feet and looked from one girl to the other as they argued, finally barking to add his view on the matter.

"What do you think, Finney?" asked Mary.

"He thinks you're being stupid, and he's telling you so," said Jody, afraid that Mary was serious and knowing she wouldn't be able to stop her from going up the tree once she set her mind to do it.

"Now, you hold Gypsy and let me get out the saw," Mary continued, as if there was nothing more to discuss.

"Mary, you can't do it! How are you going to hold on and cut at the same time?" Jody asked fearfully.

"Well, we brought a rope with us. I'll just tie myself to the tree and then my hands will be free to use the saw. Look, the trunk is really skinny up there. It won't take long at all! I'm only cutting the very top out. And besides, even if I did fall, the tree's not *that* tall, and the snow is nice and cushy! Will you stop worrying?"

*"I'm up, Jode!" Mary shouted
ecstatically from the treetop.*

Suddenly the tree looked even taller to Jody than it had before. She bit her fingernails as she watched Mary retrieve the saw and rope from the saddlebags, knowing it was pointless to continue the argument. She had made up her mind, and all Jody could do now was close her eyes and pray that Mary would get herself safely to the top of the tree and back down again.

"I'm up, Jode!" Mary shouted ecstactically from the treetop. Finnegan had not stopped barking throughout the entire tree climbing episode, and he now stood on his hind legs, front paws on the tree trunk, gazing up at Mary as if wishing he could join her there. Jody opened her eyes and looked up from her seat on Lady's back, holding Gypsy's reins in her free hand and craning her neck in order to get a better look at her reckless friend.

"Finnegan, hush!" she said, for lack of a reply to Mary, to whom she was giving the silent treatment. "You can't climb up there, so you might as well just sit down and wait. She'll be down soon, if she doesn't break her neck first."

"OK, I'm tied around the trunk!" Mary yelled. "How's it going down there?"

"Just fine, thank you," Jody replied frostily. "Will you hurry up? No, don't hurry up. Take your time. Take your time, and just don't fall out of the tree!"

The grating sound of saw teeth on wood was then heard as Mary began cutting through the upper trunk of the tree. Finnegan shook his head and sneezed as the sawdust fell into his eyes and nose. Finally deciding he had had enough, he lowered himself from the tree trunk and lay down with his chin on his paws in the snow, closing his eyes in resignation as the sawdust continued to drift down like tiny snowflakes.

"Jody! Move the ponies and Finnegan out of the way!" Mary shouted. "I'm almost through! It'll be dropping down in a minute!"

"Are you sure? It's not going to knock

you down with it, is it? Make sure you push it away from you!" Jody yelled back. "You're not tied to the part you're dropping down, are you!?"

"What do you think I am, an idiot?" Mary laughed. "Just get everybody out of the way!"

Jody hastily complied, kicking Lady to move faster as she led Gypsy away from the tree. "C'mon, Finnegan!" she whistled to the dog. "C'mon, boy, out of the way! Here comes our tree!"

"TIMBER!" Mary yelled, and just as Finnegan jumped up to follow Jody, the tree-top came tumbling down, so close that it brushed the tip of his tail as he retreated.

"Ha! Nothing to it!" Mary exulted, already untied and expertly making her way down the tree trunk, saw and rope in hand. "I knew all those years of climbing trees at the barn would pay off!"

Jody sighed with relief the instant Mary's feet touched the ground, and Finnegan wasted no time heralding Mary's return to earth, almost knocking her down as he jumped up and licked her face.

"Look at that," Mary commented proudly on her handiwork. "Have you ever seen a straighter cut? And look at the tree! It's as perfect as I thought!"

"Well, I just hope you're happy." Jody tried to sound stern but smiled in spite of herself. "Can we go home now?"

"Soon as we gather up some decorations! Did you forget about that?"

"Well, I was so busy worrying about you breaking your neck that I guess I did," Jody replied. "C'mon, let's get started."

14
Surprise in the Grain Room

MARY TIED A ROPE to the tree trunk so she could drag it back to Lucky Foot Stable behind Gypsy while Jody carefully balanced the bulging saddle bags full of the holly, rose hips, and bulrushes they had gathered to use as decorations. And despite the girls' scolding, Finnegan insisted on leaping back and forth, doing his best to bite the rope as it pulled the tree along.

"Finnegan! Cut it out!" Mary yelled. "We'll never get home if you don't get out of the way!"

Finnegan ignored Mary while Jody giggled at his antics the rest of the way home. Finally the ponies reached the farm lane and were soon snug in their stalls, munching on their hay mixed with a few carrots as Jody and Mary discussed where to set up the tree.

"It looked nice in front of the window last year," Jody suggested.

"But we should really find a new spot," Mary decided. "We can't do the same old thing every year!"

The Colonel took just that moment to add his thoughts on the matter by crowing loudly from his perch atop Lady's stall. Then he hopped down and strutted across the stable to the corner where Jody's tack trunk stood, jumped up on it, and stood like a statue, cocking his head and peering at the girls from under his floppy red comb.

"Well, that settles it then," Mary stated matter-of-factly.

"Settles what?" Jody asked.

"Where the tree should go — on your tack trunk. It's a perfect spot! The tree's not very tall, and it needs to stand on something to make it look bigger. And it'll look really nice in that corner."

"But what about my tack trunk? I need to get in there and get stuff out, you know," Jody said defensively.

"Well, c'mon. We'll get out all the stuff you really, really need and put it up on the shelf. And we'll hang your bridle on the hook by the door. It's just for a week or two!"

"Well, OK," Jody agreed. "It really is a nice spot. And I need to clean my tack trunk out anyway."

"That's the spirit! Now we just have to convince the Colonel to get himself down so we can get started."

The Colonel was encouraged to find another resting place, and the girls spent the next few hours cleaning and rearranging, setting up and decorating to their hearts' content. When the tree was finally garnished to their satisfaction, they stood back to admire their handiwork.

"Oh, Mary, it's beautiful!" Jody sighed. "Even better than last year!"

"It is!" Mary sighed contentedly. "Look how the holly and the rose hips fit together with the bulrushes. It almost looks like they grew that way."

"It sure does," came a voice from the stable door. "That is a right pretty tree."

"Willie!" Jody cried, turning to see the cowhand standing in the doorway of the stable with his hat in his hands. "Do you really think so?"

"Real nice shape. I don't recall seein' any that nice out in that old field."

"There weren't any," Jody began. "Mary climbed all the way..." And there the sentence was stopped short at the presence of Mary's hand clapped over Jody's mouth.

"Jody, Willie doesn't want to hear any boring old story about how we got the tree!

He just came in to admire it for a minute, right, Willie?" Mary asked quickly.

Willie looked from the tree to Mary with a sharp glance. "I reckon so, but I better not hear of anybody riskin' their neck just so's they could get a nice tree," he said gruffly.

"Oh, no, Willie. Not at all. Are you getting ready for milking?" Mary asked sweetly in order to change the subject.

"In a while. First I thought I'd show you somethin,' if you want to see it."

"What?" Jody asked. "Is it a new calf?"

"Lord, I hope not. No calves bein' born right now. Come on, I'll show you. That is, if you're done all your decoratin'."

Willie led Mary and Jody to the top of the barn hill and took a firm hold of the edge of the immense barn door. Mary helped him push, sliding it on its track just far enough to allow the girls to slip through. It took a moment for their eyes to adjust to the dim light inside the cavernous bank barn, and they instinctively covered their heads with their hands when the pigeons began flying back and forth overhead with a whirring of wings. At the top of this barn Mr. Mc-Murray stored his hay and straw in the enormous loft. The cows were milked in the cow stable below. The familiar, sweet smell of the hay filled their nostrils, and as the interior grew more visible, they could make out the old rope swing hanging from the rafters (much longer than the one in Lucky Foot Stable) and the door to the grain room near the back corner, to which Willie directed them now.

"Mary, look, you can still see some of our hay fort," Jody said, pointing to an odd arrangement of bales near the swing.

"Oh, yeah! It's still there from the summer!" Mary exclaimed. "We'll have to fix it up when we get time."

Willie waited patiently at the grain room door while the girls admired their fort. Only the creaking of the old wooden door as he opened it brought them out of their reverie.

"Sorry, Willie. Here we come. What could possibly be in the grain room but grain?"

"Well, if you quit your yappin' and come in here I'll show you," Willie said, walking past open grain bins full of wheat and oats waiting to be ground up for cow feed.

Willie stopped in front of the last open grain bin in the back corner of the room. The girls stood next to him and squinted into the dim corner, where a bulky, canvas-covered shape was barely visible.

"What in the world is that, Willie? And how come we've never seen it before?" Mary inquired.

"Well, I reckon you've never had much cause to come in here before," Willie said. "And this is something that hasn't been out of this room for 'bout the last twenty years."

Willie approached the curious shape and carefully untied several lengths of baling twine securing the canvas tarp. A thick cloud

But when the dust cleared, the girls drew a collective breath at the spectacle before them.

of dust flew up despite his slow drawing back of the cover, obliterating for a moment the view of what lay beneath. But when the dust cleared, the girls drew a collective breath at the spectacle before them.

Sitting in the corner of the dusty, musty old grain room, forgotten for years, was a shiny black two-seat open sleigh with red velvet seats and a delicate red pinstripe adorning the stylishly curved dashboard. Stunned into silence, the girls did not say a word as Willie leaned over and pulled from beneath the sleigh a low black tack trunk. Mary and Jody gasped again as the contents were revealed — a well-oiled black harness; a velvety brown carriage robe resplendent with embroidered red roses; and the crowning glory, a dainty set of silver sleigh bells, which jingled merrily as Willie lifted them from their resting place. It was Jody who finally found her voice.

"Oh, Willie," she whispered in awe. "Why haven't you shown us this before?"

"Well," Willie chuckled, "I near 'bout forgot it myself, but when I saw the snow today was just right for sleigh ridin', I thought about bringin' it out and givin' it a whirl. The snow has to be just right, not too deep or slushy, and the ground has to be froze."

"But, Willie, how are we going to give it a whirl?" Mary asked. "We don't have a horse that can pull it."

"Sure we do, girl. Your old plug can do it."

Mary normally became extremely offended when Willie called Gypsy an "old plug," but today she was too incredulous at his suggestion to remember to act hurt.

"My old plug?" she asked. "But she doesn't know the first thing about pulling a sleigh."

"Course she does. Any horse or pony can pull a sleigh or a carriage. Just takes a little training. In my time, I've seen many a horse pull, and they always seem to take to it better than ridin'. When the blinders go on, they go on down the road and do their job without nothin' distractin' 'em, and they seem to really enjoy it."

"But it must take a long time to teach them how!" Jody protested. "The snow will melt by then!"

"I've taught a horse to pull halfway decent in a few hours," Willie replied confidently. "And Gypsy and Lady are both pretty smart old plugs, after all."

Jody and Mary gazed wide-eyed at the beautiful little sleigh and shiny black harness and listened to the bells jingle as Willie arranged them over the pinstriped dashboard. The thought of flying swiftly down the farm lane in the crisp winter air accompanied by that bewitching sound was almost too much for the girls to bear.

"Oh, Willie — do you think we could try it? Today?" Jody asked breathlessly, afraid to breathe lest the answer be "no." Willie was usually too busy for such foolishness.

"Well, I guess I wouldn't have brought you up here to look at it if we couldn't take it out for a spin," he said gruffly. "Knowin' how you girls would bug me to death, that is."

The girls held hands and jumped up and down for joy at Willie's answer.

"Now, quit your foolishness. There's work to be done before we hitch up. Help me pick up the trunk, and we'll carry it down to the horse stable. Have to try on the harness and get the pony used to it first. You always do a dry run on the ground before you hitch up the sleigh to see how they take to it."

Before Willie had a chance to finish his sentence, Mary and Jody grabbed the leather trunk handles, and hoisting the trunk from the floor, they took off at a brisk trot toward the stable.

15
Sleigh Ride

𝓛ADY WAS LYING down in her stall, and Gypsy was dozing on her feet when the girls burst into the stable with their precious cargo followed closely by Willie and the sleigh bells. At the sudden noise, Lady pricked up her ears but made no effort to rise, and Gypsy merely turned her head to see what the commotion was about.

"Lady! Gypsy! Wake up!" Mary shouted. "You're going to learn something new this afternoon!"

At this exciting announcement, Lady lay her head on the straw, and Gypsy turned back to her corner and blew through her nose in what sounded exactly like a snore.

"You two have had plenty of time to rest up from this morning. Look what we've got for you!" Jody continued, pulling the harness collar from the trunk and holding it up for the ponies to see.

Lady's head remained down, and Gypsy simply shifted her weight from one hind leg to the other. Undeterred by the lack of reaction, Mary strode into Gypsy's stall and spoke directly in her ear.

"Gypsy Amber, you wake yourself up right now and get ready. We're embarking on a new adventure!"

"Just bring her on out here," Willie said calmly. "We'll let Lady lay still. We can teach her another day."

"She's probably too fat to fit between the shafts anyway," Mary observed. "No offense, Jody."

But Jody was too caught up in all the excitement of the moment to be offended.

"What do we do first, Willie? How do we put the harness on?" she asked eagerly.

"Not much to it, really," Willie replied. "Bring Gypsy out in the aisle here, and we'll put the collar on first. Just move real slow and act like nothin' special's happenin', and she won't mind a bit."

Mary obediently fastened a lead rope to Gypsy's halter and led her from her stall to the middle of the aisle. Willie patted her neck gently and, turning the collar upside down so that the wide end was on top, held it near Gypsy's muzzle. Gypsy reacted by sniffing it casually as if this was something she saw every day.

"You got to put the collar over her head upside down, so's it'll go over. Then you turn it right side up at her throatlatch," Willie said, demonstrating as he spoke. Gypsy didn't bat an eye as the collar went over her head.

"Now, then, after you turn it, you slide it

down her neck and rest it right in front of the withers. Now, Jody, hand me the saddle."

"The saddle?" Jody asked, looking through the tack trunk. "I don't see any saddle."

"It's not like a ridin' saddle," Willie explained patiently. "It's that kinda curved piece there with the silver hoops on top and the straps running back from it. That's it," he went on as Jody handed him the piece of harness. "Now you set the saddle right behind the withers, like so, and fasten the straps around her girth, and then the long straps go down her back, and the crupper fastens under her tail. Then your breeching straps hang down either side of her hindquarters."

Mary and Jody could tell that Willie had done this many times before as he expertly fastened the straps.

"And Gypsy doesn't mind it a bit!" Mary said incredulously. "She acts like she does this every day!"

"I told you, a horse just seems to take natural to a harness. You'll see; she's gonna learn real fast. I can tell that right now," Willie said, picking up two curved pieces of metal from the box with a long, thick leather strap attached to either side. "These are the hames, and they fasten around the collar," he instructed, strapping them on as he spoke. "And these long leather straps are the traces. They go along her sides and attach to the sleigh. Now you just have your bridle and these long reins, called lines, to put on and you're ready to go."

Gypsy stood dead still, transfixed by Willie's calming voice and his gentle hands on her sides as he fastened the girth straps, and she willingly opened her mouth for the bit when he held it near her muzzle.

"Willie, she likes it," Jody said quietly, fearful of breaking the spell. "Do you think she'll mind when she feels the sleigh back there?"

"Well, we're goin' to try her out first without the sleigh," Willie replied, placing the dangling traces across Gypsy's back so they wouldn't drag on the ground.

"How are you going to do that?" Mary asked curiously.

"You just watch and see," Willie said as he led Gypsy out the stable door and over to the packed snow of the long farm lane. "Now, Mary, you stand at her head."

Mary did as she was told, and Willie walked behind Gypsy and took up the lines, one in each hand. Gypsy pricked up her ears and looked down the lane as though eager to get going.

"Willie!" Mary exclaimed suddenly. "We forgot the sleigh bells!"

"That we did," chuckled Willie. "Jody, you run and get'em. Might as well get her used to the sound now."

Jody was back in no time with the bells jingling in her hand. "Can I put them on?" she asked eagerly.

"I reckon," Willie said. "Just be careful

not to spook her. Be real slow when you put 'em around her neck."

Jody was so careful with the bells that they hardly jingled as she placed them just in front of Gypsy's withers. At the unfamiliar feel of the soft leather settling at the base of her neck, she shook her head, setting the bells to jingling. Jody and Mary laughed together when Gypsy turned to see what all the commotion was.

"She's gonna do fine," Willie said softly. "You see how she turned her head to look, but she didn't take a step? She knows what to do. Now, Mary, you just stay at her head and wait 'til I gather up the lines."

Willie moved quickly but quietly, taking a line in each hand and standing behind Gypsy at just about the place he would be if he were seated in the sleigh.

"Now, Mary, I'm just going to tap her a little with the lines. You can let go of her head," he instructed. Mary stood back and grabbed Jody's arm, and the girls stood breathlessly awaiting Gypsy's reaction to this strange new sensation of being urged forward with no weight on her back.

"C'mon, Gypsy, you can do it," Jody whispered, squeezing Mary's hand nervously.

The girls needn't have worried for a minute, as Gypsy moved off at a brisk walk without a hitch, Willie clucking gently behind. Willie walked Gypsy to the end of the lane, turned her around, and then with a cluck and a "Git up!" urged Gypsy into an easy trot back toward the girls, sleigh bells jingling merrily in the still afternoon air.

"Look at Willie trotting along behind!" Mary giggled. "I never knew he could move that fast!"

"I think there's a lot of things about Willie that we never knew," Jody replied, "and he sure hasn't gone out of his way to tell us."

They were quiet then until Gypsy arrived back at her starting place, coming to a gentle halt with a slight tug of the lines.

"She did it, Willie! She did it!" Mary exclaimed. "Can we hook her up now?"

"Now, just hold yer horses," Willie said patiently. "It's a lot different when she feels the weight of the sleigh behind her. Let her just stand and be quiet for a minute. Then we'll ground drive her up the barn hill and get the sleigh out."

"We'll get it out, Willie!" shouted Jody, pulling on Mary's coat sleeve. "C'mon, Mare, we'll go up and pull it out of the barn, and it'll be all ready when Willie and Gypsy get there."

"Be careful gettin' it through the door!" Willie shouted after them, shaking his head and chuckling as he watched them tear around the bend to the barn.

Willie was out of breath when he and Gypsy arrived at the barn doors, having driven her on foot around the bend and to the top of the barn hill at a brisk walk. Greeting him there were Mary and Jody and the jaunty black sleigh, all ready to hitch up.

"Look, Willie! We figured out how to hook the shafts to the sleigh!" Jody said proudly.

"Good thing," said Willie brusquely. "It's almost milkin' time, and I don't have much more time for this foolishness."

At that, Willie turned Gypsy and expertly backed her until her hindquarters were in position in front of the two long shafts of the sleigh. Before Jody and Mary knew what had happened, the traces were fastened to the shafts and the tugs hooked up while Gypsy stood like a statue.

"Now, Mary, you stand at her head again while I get in and get the lines straight," Willie ordered.

"Oh, Willie, can I get in with you?" Jody implored.

"Hey, what about me?" Mary chimed in.

"Neither one of you are goin' to ride until I drive her once and see how she'll do. She might just take off and flip the whole daggone thing over," Willie said ominously, but the girls knew he didn't really think Gypsy would do any such thing. "Now, Mary, you can turn loose of her head."

Mary shut her eyes and said a short but fervent prayer before turning loose of Gypsy's driving bridle. But Gypsy didn't move a muscle, waiting for Willie's command.

"Git up, girl, move on," Willie said softly, clucking and slapping the lines gently on Gypsy's hindquarters. "Now, see, if I had my driving whip, I wouldn't be using the lines to get her moving," he instructed the girls. "I'd just give her a little tap with the end of the whip. That's the proper way."

But Gypsy didn't know anything about a whip. She just knew that WIllie was urging her on, and she took a few steps forward. But just as soon as she started off, she stopped dead and stood, as if waiting for the next command. Willie just chuckled.

"Willie, what's wrong? Why did she stop?" Mary wondered. "Did you tell her to?"

"No, that's what they often do when they go forward for the first time and feel the weight of the collar pressin' on their shoulders. They think when they feel that pressure in front they're s'posed to stop. Watch now; she'll get the feel of it in a minute."

Willie clucked to Gypsy again, and she started forward only to stop again after a few steps. This time she turned her head and looked back at Willie as if to ask what in the world he wanted her to do.

"She's confused, Willie!" Mary laughed. "She doesn't know if you want her to stop or go!"

"Just hold on now..." Willie answered, slapping the lines on Gypsy's hindquarters a little harder. "Git up," he urged, and this time Gypsy started forward, and with the continued slap of the lines, walked on without hesitation.

"Good girl, Gypsy! Good girl!" Mary called after her, and when Willie urged

Gypsy into a trot, the girls took off trotting as well, skipping gaily after the sleigh as Gypsy snorted and tossed her head to the tune of the jingling bells. Willie drove Gypsy to the end of the lane, turned her without a hitch and drove back to the stable. Dusk was approaching when Willie finally said it was safe for the girls to climb into the back seat behind him.

The setting sun cast a ghostly glow on the crust of snow along the farm lane, and the only sound came from Gypsy blowing softly through her nostrils, her warm breath making wispy clouds in the frosty air. Hoofprints and narrow tracks from the sleigh's runners marked the snow on the lane where Willie had driven Gypsy up and down.

"Oh, Willie, I'm just going to die," Jody breathed as she arranged the thick brown carriage robe over Mary's legs and her own.

"Me too," agreed Mary, squeezing Jody's arm. "Willie, we've got all the blanket. Do you want it?"

An involuntary squeal burst from both girls' lips,
followed by a bubbling of delighted laughter.

"No, ma'am, I'm right warm. And that's called a robe, not a blanket. And what do you mean, you're gonna die? It's just an old sleigh ride," Willie said, trying to sound nonchalant. "And it's gonna be a short one. I'm late for milkin' now. The cows'll think I died, not you."

"We know, Willie. Thanks ever so for taking us! When you teach us to drive, then we won't have to bother you anymore!" Mary said sweetly.

Willie just shook his head as he clucked to Gypsy once more, urging her smoothly into a practiced trot as though she had been pulling a sleigh her whole life. An involuntary squeal burst from both girls' lips, followed by a bubbling of delighted laughter as the sleigh glided swiftly down the lane.

"What're you laughin' at?" Willie asked, trying to sound annoyed.

"Willie, this is the best ever!!" Mary replied breathlessly.

"Best ever, is it?" Willie responded. "Hmmph. Just an old sleigh ride," he repeated under his breath. And then Willie grinned like a youngster in spite of himself.

"Willie, you know you like it!" Jody squealed, opening her mouth wide to take in big gulps of the crisp, cold air.

The remainder of the ride was relished in contented silence, words being inadequate to express the individual emotions of the three riders. Willie reined Gypsy in at the end of the lane and they sat, silently absorbing the still white beauty of the wintry twilight. Suddenly, Willie patted the seat next to him.

"Mary, why don't you come up here and try driving your old plug back up the lane. It's past milkin' time, and you've got to git me back to the barn right quick."

Mary's mouth opened wide and then shut again. She looked at Willie without a word.

"You can do it, Mary. Just turn her at the walk like you would if you were ridin', and then straighten her up and trot her on up the lane. She knows your feel already. You won't have no trouble. And I'm right here in case you do. And Jody, you can drive next time when we teach Lady."

"OK, Willie, I don't mind," Jody sighed, content to ride along and happy for her best friend.

Mary settled herself in the front seat, took up the lines and guided Gypsy gently to the right until they faced the barn. Then with a, "Get up, girl!" they were off. As the dashing little sleigh made its way along in the snow, jingling all the way, Mary and Jody thought that nothing in the world, no adventure thereafter in their lives — no matter how wonderful, would ever be as happy and sweet as that very moment.

Of course, at that moment there was no way to predict that very soon they would be proven wrong.

16
Will the Animals Speak?

CHRISTMAS EVE ARRIVED at last, and Mary and Jody bustled about Lucky Foot Stable, preparing for the special night. Lady and Gypsy stood in their stalls, nibbling their hay, as their breath formed silvery clouds in the chilly air. The little tree with all of its natural decorations stood festively on Jody's tack trunk and was lit only by the full moon shining through the window, illuminating several brightly wrapped gifts beneath its lowest branches. Colonel Sanders cocked his head as he roosted on the top board of Lady's stall, watching as Jody swept the aisle and Mary broke open a bale of straw to make a bed in the far corner. Finnegan immediately took advantage of the situation by flopping down in the midst of the bedding and resting his chin on his paws.

Suddenly Mary ceased her activity and looked solemnly at Jody.

"Now, Jody, you remember our vow," she said. "We have to be diligent, you know. Not like last year."

Jody nodded, recalling the disappointment of last year's Christmas Eve in the stable.

"Of course I remember, Mare," she said, holding her broom still and raising her right hand. "We will not fall asleep. We will be awake at midnight. And if the animals speak, we will hear them."

Mary simply nodded and went back to fluffing the straw.

Jody, of course, was talking about the

legend, passed down throughout the centuries, which declares that on Christmas Eve at the stroke of midnight, the animals miraculously begin to speak of the wondrous morning on that first Christmas Day, which was witnessed firsthand by their own ancestors in the lowly stable in Bethlehem. Mary had read about the legend in a book and had recounted it to Jody in the weeks before Christmas last year. The girls had begged and pleaded at home, finally receiving permission to stay in the stable overnight, only to fall asleep before midnight, missing the wondrous sound of their ponies speaking to each other. This year, if the miracle was to happen, they were determined to be awake for it.

"Finney, you're just going to have to move!" Mary admonished the sleepy dog, laughing as he yawned and batted at her hand with his paw. "I've got to fix up the straw so it will make a nice cushion under our sleeping bags."

"Don't make it too comfortable, Mare," cautioned Jody. "If it's too comfortable we'll fall asleep for sure."

"But, Jody, we're not even going to let ourselves lay down until after midnight. That way we'll be sure to stay awake. We'll just have to sit up and sing carols or something."

"Well," Jody said shyly, and then stopped.

"Well, what?" Mary asked curiously. "What are you thinking?"

"Well, I was thinking, we could... we could... open our presents!" Jody replied, a little too quickly.

"Jody, you know we never open our presents until Christmas Day. Don't be silly!" Then, seeing the pained expression on Jody's face, she stopped and put her hands on her hips. "Now, would you mind telling me what you really want to do? We still have three hours till midnight!"

"Well, I didn't want to tell you because I'm too embarrassed. But, I wrote something, and I brought it tonight so we could read it. It's about, you know, the legend and everything."

Even in the dimly lit stable, Mary could see that Jody's face had turned beet red. She smiled at her friend and lowered her voice almost to a whisper.

"Well, why didn't you say so? Of course I want to hear it. Why don't you get it out and let me see it? Do you want to read it out loud, or should I read it to myself?"

Jody reached into her knapsack without a word and pulled out a small white paper, which she had folded over and over until it was the size of a dollar. She gripped it in her hand for a moment, then held it out for Mary to take. But before Mary had the chance, she pulled it back and opened it quickly.

"No, I'll read it to you," she said courageously, suffering the acute embarrassment every new writer feels when faced with reading their own work for others to hear. "It's a poem, and it's really not very good. But it just came to me the other day when I was thinking about hearing the animals talk."

"So, let's hear it already!" Mary began loudly, but then remembering how difficult this was for Jody, she lowered her voice again. "I'm sure it's great, Jode! Go ahead. No, wait. Stand over here so Lady and Gypsy and the Colonel can hear. And Finnegan, get over here, you lazy dog. Jody has a poem for us all to hear." And Mary cleared her own throat as though about to read the poem herself.

Lady and Gypsy hung their heads over the front of their stalls, and the Colonel gazed down from his perch. The obedient Finnegan padded over and lay down at Mary's feet, looking expectantly up at Jody. It really did seem as if every creature, man and beast, in the stable was listening as Jody smiled shyly and shook out the paper, holding it in front of her face to hide her embarrassment.

"OK, now remember — it's not very

good. It's called, "The Animals Spoke." And
she began to read aloud:

The legend was known throughout the land
By every woman, child, and man
That on Christmas Eve in Bethlehem
The animals spoke,
The animals spoke.

In the stable at midnight, upon the hay
That fed the animals every day
The Christ Child was born, and there He lay
While the animals spoke,
The animals spoke.

The first to speak was the woolly sheep
Whispering low, for the Babe was asleep
And Mary said, "hush," the quiet to keep
While the animals spoke,
The animals spoke.

"I will give of my wool for the tiny Child

Comfort and warmth I'll gladly provide
In cloth from my back He will ever abide
And remember me,
Remember me."

"I'll give Him my milk," said the
    cow from her stall
"As He grows to a man, so handsome and tall
He'll never go hungry while preaching to all
He'll depend on me,
He'll depend on me."

"But He'll need me as well," said
    the donkey so proud
"For one day I'll carry Him safe
    through the crowd
Triumphantly into Jerusalem town
On my back He will ride,
On my back He will ride."

As the shepherds worshipped the Holy One,
The animals' work had just begun.
"God made us all to care for His Son,"

They whispered with pride,
They whispered with pride.

Now the legend to this very day we recall
That on Christmas Eve, just as
midnight falls,
In Remembrance of Him, who saved us all,
The animals speak,
The animals speak.

When Jody finished reading, the stable was as hushed as the world outside, where a light snow had begun to fall. Mary stood with her mouth open, but no sound emerged. The Colonel ruffled his feathers quietly, and Lady shook her head up and down. Finnegan lay with his chin resting on Mary's foot. The quiet was finally interrupted by Jody herself.

"Mary? Was it really bad? What did you think? You can tell me honestly." And she waited breathlessly for Mary's reply.

"*Well, Jody Stafford, that was just
about the best thing J ever heard in my life!*"

Mary shut her mouth and swallowed once before she spoke, and then her voice came almost in a whisper.

"Well, Jody Stafford, that was just about the best thing I ever heard in my life! I didn't know you could do that! Why didn't you tell me you wrote poetry? We have to send this somewhere and get it published, and then you'll be famous!"

"Oh, Mare, I don't write poetry. This is the very first poem I ever wrote! I told you, it just came to me when I thought about the animals speaking, and about how God didn't just make us to take care of the animals, He made the animals to take care of us too. That's all. Then writing the poem was easy."

"Easy for you, maybe. But I don't even know any grownups that could've written that!" And as if in agreement, Lady nickered softly and shook her head up and down again.

"See, even Lady thinks so," Mary laughed.

Jody, glowing from Mary's praise, smiled shyly and went to Lady, and laying her head against the softness of Lady's neck, sighed a deep sigh of contentment.

"Here, Jody, give me the poem, and we'll find a place of honor for it," Mary suggested. "I know. We'll put it right on top of the tree. We never really had a tree topper." Carefully rolling the paper into a scroll, she took a red ribbon from one of the gifts beneath the tree.

Jody watched as she arranged the ribbon around the poem, making a bow in front, and then tied the dangling ends around the top branch.

"There," Mary announced. "It's perfect. Maybe in the morning, after we hear the animals speak, we'll read it again."

Jody impulsively gave her friend a hug. "Thanks for liking it, Mary. You've inspired me! Maybe I'll write some more someday."

"Well, you have to. Then, after you become rich and famous, we'll buy our own farm and let Lady and Gypsy go out to pasture in their old age."

This time it was Gypsy who nickered as if agreeing with every word.

"Alright, troops. Now what shall we do to keep busy?" Mary asked loudly. "I propose a walk in the moonlight. How about it, Fin?"

So the girls walked out into the brilliantly lit night, crunching in the snow while Finnegan bounded along. They strolled down the lane and then up to the barn to visit the sleigh. On their way back to the stable, they had a snowball fight and built a snowman with frozen horse droppings for eyes. Of course, Mary had to get one of Willie's hats from the cow stable to put on the snowman's head in an effort to make it look like Willie. By the time the trio got back to Lucky Foot, there was still an hour to go until midnight.

"Now, I propose we sing a few carols," Mary suggested after they had entered the stable, knocked the snow off their boots, and checked on the ponies.

"Well, let's get into our sleeping bags, at least," Jody said with a yawn. "My feet are freezing! And as long as we're singing, we can't fall asleep."

"Good plan," Mary agreed. "C'mon, Finnegan. You can lay down between us and keep us warm."

The boots then came off altogether, and the girls snuggled down in their sleeping bags with straw for pillows as they awaited the stroke of midnight. Finnegan gladly lay between them, licking first one face and then the other while the girls giggled and pretended they didn't like it.

"OK, Finney, what shall we sing?" Mary asked the dog earnestly. "We have to keep you awake too, so we can hear if you have anything to say at midnight."

"My favorite Christmas song is *Do You Hear What I Hear?*" Jody confessed. "But I don't think I know all the words."

"Oh, I think I do," Mary offered. "I know them, but I never get them in the right order.

Does the night wind ask the little lamb if he knows what he sees, or hears? And does the star have a tail as big as a kite, or a tree?"

"Maybe we'd better skip that one," Jody laughed. "How about an easy one, like *We Three Kings?*"

"OK, I know. I'll sing the first three words, then you sing the next three, and we'll go on like that, and then we'll sing the chorus together!" And this is what they did:

Mary: "We three kings..."

Jody: "of Orient are..."

Mary: "bearing gifts we..."

Jody: "traverse afar..."

"Wait. Is *afar* one word or two?" Mary demanded.

"I don't know. Does it matter?" Jody yawned again.

"Well, if we really want to each sing three words, it does."

"Maybe we should just sing the chorus. I'm not sure I know all the words to the rest of it anyway," Jody suggested.

"OK, here goes," Mary said. And they sang together: "'Star of wonder, star of night, star with royal beauty bright. Westward leading, still proceeding, guide us with thy perfect light.'"

On the last line, Mary suddenly realized she was singing by herself.

"Jody?" she said. No reply. And when she looked, she discovered that Jody and Finnegan had fallen fast asleep in the middle of the song.

"Well, I'll just let her sleep a little bit," she said to herself. "I'll wake her up just before midnight, which is in precisely... fifteen minutes!"

Then, after taking one last look at her watch, Mary shut her eyes for just an instant.

And in that instant, she fell fast asleep herself.

17
Star of Wonder

THE LIGHTLY FALLING snow had become a blizzard. Jody and Lady were far from the barn in the pitch dark, the wind was howling, and Finnegan struggled along beside them through the deep drifts as they tried desperately to make their way back to the barn. Jody looked frantically for some kind of landmark that might help her find her way. Suddenly, a whole troop of snowmen with black eyes and farm caps appeared before them, beckoning them with their icy arms. Finnegan whined fearfully, and Lady whinnied and reared at the terrifying sight, throwing Jody off into a snowdrift that completely enveloped her, trapping her arms and legs and threatening to cover her head.

"Jody! Jody!" Mary was yelling in her ear and shaking her arm.

Thank goodness Mary is here to rescue me!

"Jody, wake up!" Mary said frantically. "You've gotten yourself all tangled up in your sleeping bag, and you're having a nightmare!"

Jody stopped struggling and opened her eyes. Mary was glaring down at her, half frightened, half angry.

"And not only that, we went to sleep before midnight!" Mary continued glumly. "Look, it's almost dawn!"

Jody rubbed her eyes and looked up to see the half-light of the rising sun peeking through the dusty window of the stable.

"Oh, no!" she cried. "We couldn't have

done it again! What happened, Mare? I don't even remember falling asleep!"

Before Mary could reply, the sound of Finnegan whining and pawing at the dirt floor in front of Lady's stall and Lady nickering restlessly caught the girls' attention.

"Lady and Finnegan!" Jody cried. "I heard them in my dream! We were lost, and we couldn't find our way back, and we saw these snowmen, and Finney was whining and Lady was whinnying just like they are now. I think that was what started to wake me up!"

"Could've fooled me," Mary said grumpily. "Now, what is all this racket about, anyway?" And she jumped out of her sleeping bag and strode across the stable to see for herself while Jody, feeling miserable for having slept through another Christmas Eve midnight, covered her head with her sleeping bag.

"Finnegan, what in the world is the matter with you?" Mary began, looking down at the distressed dog as he continued to scratch and whine.

"There's nothing to be whining abou..." Mary stopped short in the middle of her sentence. Jody looked up curiously from her sleeping bag to see Mary standing completely still as she looked into Lady's stall.

"Mary? What is it, Mare?" Jody asked.

"Oh. Oh. Oh," Mary gasped. "Oh!"

"What?" Jody asked again.

When Mary didn't reply, Jody scrambled from her sleeping bag and ran to Lady's stall. She stood on tiptoe and looked through the two top boards.

And then it was her turn to gasp in shock.

In the shadowy light of the early sun's rays sifting through the window of the stall stood Lady in her usual place by the manger. The Colonel looked down from his regular place on the top board, and Gypsy hung her head over her own stall door, as she usually did.

But standing next to Lady, knee deep in the bright bed of straw, wobbling on shaky legs and blinking curiously at the girls through long dark lashes, stood a beautiful black and white, newly born pinto foal with a perfect white star on its forehead. Lady, the proud mother, nickered softly and nuzzled her baby protectively as Mary and Jody stared in disbelief at the miraculous sight. Then, without a word, Jody slowly and quietly opened the door of the stall and went in.

"Jody," Mary whispered through the stall boards as Jody kneeled silently in the straw near the baby. "Jode, do you think it would be all right if I came in, too?"

Jody looked up at Mary through the tears that had sprung to her eyes as she knelt near the baby and nodded her head. "Of course, Mary," she whispered back. "I'm sorry I didn't invite you in right away. I'm just... just... I can't believe it! How could we not have known?"

Mary slowly entered the stall and knelt beside Jody. The foal blinked and fearlessly snuffled at her hair before turning toward

"Jody, it's a miracle. We didn't get to hear the
animals speak, but this is just as big of a miracle!"

Lady and nuzzling for milk. The girls watched in delight as the baby nursed energetically.

"Jody, it's a miracle," Mary said breathlessly. "We didn't get to hear the animals speak, but this is just as big of a miracle!"

"I just can't believe I didn't know," Jody said once again. "I mean, I noticed Lady was getting fat and kind of lazy, but I didn't know why!"

"I know. I kept teasing you about that, but I didn't get it either! And look, it's a boy. And his star... it's just like his father's! The Black Stallion... remember?"

"I can't believe Willie didn't know, either. He was in the paddock with Lady and the stallion. When he saw Lady getting fat, he should have figured it out!" Jody declared.

"Maybe he did. Maybe he just wanted us to be surprised," Mary said. "When he gets here for milking, we'll ask him."

There was silence then as the girls took in all that had happened. They watched as the determined little foal nuzzled and pushed at

Lady's flank for more milk. Then, satisfied at last, he turned and blinked at them once again, tiny droplets of milk adorning his whiskers. Mary burst out laughing so loudly that the frightened foal fell back on his haunches and down on the straw in a heap.

"Oh, baby, I'm so sorry," Mary laughed and whispered all at once. Jody held her sides, her face beet red from trying not to laugh out loud as Mary had.

"Mary, we've got to name him," Jody said at last through her happy tears. "We can't go on calling him baby."

"We do," Mary agreed. "Let's think."

"I know already," Jody said. "I thought of it right away, but I didn't say anything."

Jody grew quiet while Mary looked at her expectantly. And still she said nothing. Finally Mary could stand it no longer.

"Well, are you going to tell me or not?" Mary insisted.

"I'm afraid you won't like it," Jody said shyly.

"Well, how am I going to know if you don't tell me?" Mary said impatiently. "You said I wasn't going to like your poem, either, remember? So tell me!"

"Well, as soon as I saw the star, I remembered the song we sang before we fell asleep."

"We Three Kings?" Mary said skeptically. "I don't know, Jode, that's kind of a weird name for a foal."

"No," Jody laughed. "Remember the chorus? 'Star of wonder, star of night...'"

"Star of Wonder!" Mary gasped. "Star of Wonder! Jody, that's brilliant! We can call him Star for short!"

And then, as if satisfied with his new name, Star of Wonder, full from Lady's milk, stretched out in the straw, and resting his drowsy head on Jody's leg, he blinked once more, breathed a contented sigh, and fell fast asleep.

Glossary of Horse Terms

Bale – In stable terms, a bale is a closely packed bundle of either hay or straw (see definitions) measuring about two by three feet, weighing about forty pounds and tied with two strings lengthwise. When the strings are cut, the bale can be shaken loose and either fed, in the case of hay, or used for stall bedding, in the case of straw.

Baling Twine – The term used for the thick yellow string that is tied around a bale.

Bank Barn – A barn that is built into the side of a hill so that the hill forms a "ramp" leading into the upper part of the barn, where hay and straw may be stored; the bottom floor of the barn is used for milking the cows if it is a dairy barn, or it may have stalls for the purpose of sheltering other animals.

Barn Swallow – A small, blue-black bird with a rusty-colored breast and throat and forked tail; found all over North America and Europe, these friendly birds like to build their nests in barns and eat insects.

Bay – A common color seen in horses and ponies. The body is reddish-brown with black mane, tail, and lower legs.

Bit – The metal piece on the bridle inserted into the mouth of a horse that provides communication between the rider and horse.

Blinders – A leather attachment to a driving bridle designed to restrict the vision of the horse from the rear and sides and to focus the vision forward.

Breeching Straps – An attachment to the driving harness which fits across the hindquarters of the horse about twelve inches below the dock of the tail and fastens to the shafts of the cart. These straps help to keep the cart from hitting the horse when going down a hill.

Bridle – The leather headgear, with a metal bit, which is placed on the head of a horse to enable the rider to control the horse.

Canter – A three-beat gait of the horse that could be called a "collected gallop." It is slightly faster and not so "bouncy" as a trot.

Carriage – A horse-drawn, four-wheeled vehicle.

Carriage Robe – A heavy blanket about five feet square, which is used to cover the legs of the occupant and provides warmth while riding in a carriage or sleigh.

Chestnut – A common color found in horses and ponies. The coat is basically red, in varying shades on different horses. The mane and tail are the same color as the body.

Cluck – The "clicking" sound a rider or driver makes from the corner of the mouth to urge a horse forward. Also the sound a chicken makes when communicating.

Collar – The oval, leather piece of harness that fits around the horse's neck to which the hames and traces are attached. The collar allows the horse to pull the carriage by pushing his weight against the collar and walking forward.

Corncob – The inner segment of an ear of

corn to which the corn kernels are attached. The horse eats the kernels but not the cob.

Crop – A short leather riding whip carried by the rider and used lightly to encourage the horse to move forward.

Crosstie – The method of tying a horse squarely in the aisle or stall by which a rope is clipped to both sides of the halter. When a horse is crosstied, he cannot move away from the rider during grooming and saddling.

Crupper – The part of the driving harness that fastens around the top of the tail to help keep the saddle and breeching straps in place.

Dismount – The action of getting down from a horse and onto the ground.

Dock – The bone in the horse's tail, which is formed of the lowest vertebrae of the spine.

Dollar Bareback – A game on horseback in which a dollar is placed under the knee of the rider while riding bareback, and then the riders must walk, trot, and even canter around the ring without losing the dollar. The last person with the dollar still under their knee wins all the dollars.

Eaves – The overhanging lower edge of a roof.

Field horse – Another term for a work horse; a horse that is hitched to equipment and performing work in a field, such as plowing or planting.

Flake – A section of hay that is taken from a bale for feeding, usually about six inches wide and two feet square. There are usually about ten flakes of hay in a whole bale.

Flaxen – A cream-colored mane and tail sometimes found on chestnut horses and always found on palominos. If a chestnut has a flaxen mane and tail, he is known as a "flaxen chestnut."

Foal – A young, unweaned horse or pony of either gender. When the horse or pony is "weaned" or separated from its mother, it is called a "weanling."

Gallop – A fast, four-beat gait where all four of the horse's feet strike the ground separately.

Grain – Harvested cereals or other edible seeds, including oats, corn, wheat, and barley. Horses and ponies often eat a mixture of grains, vitamins, minerals, and molasses called "sweet feed."

Gray – A common color found in horses and ponies. A gray horse is born black and gradually lightens with age from a steel-gray color to almost white.

Graze – The act of eating grass. Horses and ponies will graze continually when turned out on good pasture.

Groom – To groom a horse is to clean and brush his coat, comb his mane and tail, and pick the dirt from his hooves. A person known as a "groom" goes along on a horse show or horse race to help with grooming, tacking up, or anything else that needs to be done.

Ground drive – The act of driving a horse in full harness but not hooked to a cart or carriage. A person steers the horse by walking behind the horse and holding the long reins. This is a method used to train a horse to drive.

Gully – A trench worn in the earth by running water after a rain.

Gymkhana – A horse show made up of

games on horseback, including games defined elsewhere in this glossary.

Halter – Also known as a "head collar," a halter is made of rope, leather, or nylon and is placed on the head of the horse and used for leading or tying him. The halter has no bit, but it has a metal ring that rests under the chin of the horse to which you attach a lead rope.

Hames – The metal pieces of the driving harness that fasten around the collar and are attached to the traces.

Hard brush – A grooming tool used on a horse or pony. A brush, resembling a scrub brush, usually with firm bristles made of nylon, used to brush dried mud or dirt from the coat and legs.

Harness – The collection of leather straps, bridle, reins, and collar that is placed on the horse or pony and attached to a cart, sleigh, or carriage.

Haunches – Another term for the hindquarters of a horse or pony.

Hay – Grass or other herbage that is cut in the field and allowed to dry over several days and then usually baled and stored in a barn to be used as feed for animals.

Haynet – A nylon or rope net, which is stuffed with loose hay and tied at the top and then hung in a stall or trailer to allow the animal to eat from it.

Hindquarters – The rear of the horse or pony, including the back legs.

Hitch up – Attaching a horse or pony to a cart, carriage, or sleigh through the use of harness straps.

Hoof pick – The grooming tool used to clean the dirt and gravel from the hooves of a horse or pony.

Hooves – The hard covering of the foot of a horse or pony. The hooves must be cleaned before and after riding and trimmed every six weeks (or so) to keep them from growing too long.

Jump standards – The wooden or vinyl upright supports on either side of the jump that hold the jump cups onto which the jump rails or poles are placed.

Keyhole race – A game on horseback in which a pattern in the shape of a keyhole is painted or limed on the ground. The rider gallops the horse or pony to the end of the pattern and back again without stepping outside the lines. The fastest time wins.

Lead rope – A length of cotton or nylon rope

of about six feet with a snap attached to the end. The rope is used to lead the horse or pony.

Leg up – The action of helping someone mount by grasping their bended left knee and hoisting them up and onto the back of a horse or pony.

Leather conditioner – An oily or creamy substance that is rubbed into leather to help keep it from drying out and cracking.

Lines – Another term for the long reins used with a harness to drive a horse.

Loft – The large area in the top of a barn used to store bales of hay and straw.

Mane – The long hair that grows on the crest (top) of a horse or pony's neck and hangs over on one side or the other.

Manger – A wooden box with an open top,

usually attached to the wall of a stall, used for feeding grain to a horse or pony.

Mare – A female horse or pony three years of age or older.

Mare's tails – Also known as cirrus clouds, these are wispy cloud formations that actually look like the long flowing tail of a horse or pony.

Milkers – The equipment that is attached to the cow's teats in order to draw the milk out of the udder through a pulsing action.

Milk house – The small building attached to a dairy barn where the milk ends up in a cooling tank.

Mustang – A native breed of horse that is found mostly in the western plains and lives in the wild, although many mustangs have been caught and tamed for riding.

Muzzle – The lower end of the nose of a horse or pony, which includes the nostrils, lips, and chin.

Neat's-foot oil – A type of oil used to condition leather to keep it from drying out and cracking.

Nicker – A low, quiet sound made by a horse or pony in greeting or when wanting to be fed.

Obstacle course – A game on horseback involving various obstacles around which the rider and horse or pony must maneuver, such as going over a bridge, trotting between poles, opening gates while mounted, etc.

Paddock – A fenced area, smaller than a field, used for enclosing animals for limited exercise.

Pinto – A horse or pony of a solid coat color with white patches or markings on various parts of the body. The mane and tail may be various colors.

Pole bending – A game on horseback that involves riding a horse or pony through a slalom pattern in and out of vertically positioned poles without touching the poles. Fastest time wins.

Pony – A pony measures below 14.3 hands from the bottom of the hoof to the withers. (see definition). A hand equals four inches. 14.3 hands and above is considered a horse.

Reins – The leather straps of the bridle attached to the bit and held by the rider to guide and control the horse.

Ringmaster – The person at a horse show who assists the judge in the ring and helps any rider who falls; also may replace rails that may be knocked from a jump by a horse.

Saddle – A saddle is placed on a horse or pony's back, secured by a girth, and is a leather, padded seat for the rider; or part of a harness that is placed on the horse or pony's back behind the withers.

Saddlebags – Two leather pouches attached to each other by a wide piece of leather that drapes over the saddle or withers of the horse, or sometimes behind the saddle, to allow the rider to carry supplies on the trail.

Saddle rack – A metal or wooden frame attached to the wall or stall on which to hang the saddle.

Salt block – A square, compact brick made of salt and placed in the field or stall; the horse licks the block, which provides him with salt and other minerals.

Shafts – The poles attached to a carriage,

sleigh, or cart between which a horse or pony is hitched to pull the vehicle.

Sleigh – A horse-drawn vehicle that does not have wheels, but "runners" for gliding over snow or ice.

Slip knot – A type of knot, also known as "quick release," which can be quickly and easily untied in case of a problem, such as the horse or pony falling down or getting hung up.

Soft brush – A brush made for grooming a horse or pony's coat and face; it is the same shape as a scrub brush but has softer, longer bristles.

Spook – An action of the horse or pony in which they shy away nervously from something they are not familiar with.

Stallion – A male horse or pony that has

not been neutered and may be used for re-
productive purposes.

Star – Any white mark on the forehead of a
horse or pony, located above a (imaginary)
line running from eye to eye.

Straw – The material used for bedding in a
stall; it consists of the stalks of grain from
which the grain has been removed and the
stalks baled. It should be bright yellow and
not dusty.

Tack – Equipment used in riding and driving
horses or ponies, such as saddles, bridles,
harnesses, etc.

Tack box – A container with a handle used
to transport grooming tools, bridle, and other
equipment to horse shows or other events.

Tack trunk– A large trunk usually kept in
the stable that contains the equipment used

by the rider, such as bridles, grooming tools, the saddle, lead ropes, medicines, etc.

Throatlatch – The narrow strap of the bridle, which goes under the horse's throat and is used to secure the bridle to the head.

Traces – The thick leather straps on the harness that attach the hames to the carriage and allow the horse or pony to pull the vehicle.

Trot – A rapid, two-beat gait in which the front foot and the opposite hind foot take off at the same time and strike the ground simultaneously.

Trough – A long, shallow receptacle used for feeding or watering animals.

Tugs – Common name for the leather straps attaching the shafts to the breeching straps of a horse-drawn vehicle.

Udder – The mammary glands of a cow where the four teats are attached and the milk is produced.

Wash stall – An enclosed area, usually inside the stable, with hot and cold running water where a horse or pony may be cross-tied and bathed.

Whinny – A high pitched, loud call of a horse.

Winter coat – The longish hair that a horse or pony naturally grows in the winter to protect him from the cold. In the spring, the winter coat "sheds out" and the body becomes sleek again with a short hair coat.

Withers – The ridge at the base of the neck and between the shoulders of a horse or pony. The saddle sits on the horse's back behind the withers, and a horse or pony's height is measured from the ground to the top of the withers.

Tailwinds Farm

Visitors can relax in country comfort at our lovingly restored Victorian farmhouse — a bed & breakfast which has been featured in *The New York Times*, the *Baltimore Sun*, and on *Good Morning America*.

Conveniently located between Philadelphia, Baltimore, and Washington, D.C., the rolling hills of northeast Maryland beckon horse lovers of all ages to come and enjoy a wide variety of activities — guided trail rides through Fair Hill state park, pony rides for the little ones, carriage rides, riding lessons, summer camp, horse shows, and even special holiday events!

To learn more about the bed & breakfast and stables at Tailwinds Farm, visit our website at www.fairwindsstables.com or call us at 410-658-8187.

About the Author

JoAnn Dawson with Painted Warrior

JoAnn Dawson has always loved horses and has owned them since childhood. She, her husband Ted, and their two sons live in Maryland on a horse farm where they operate a bed & breakfast and offer riding lessons, carriage rides, horse shows, and a summer camp.

JoAnn teaches Equine Science at a local college, is an actress and animal wrangler for film and television, and has enjoyed competing regionally over the years on her American Paint horse, Painted Warrior.

Books in the

STABLE SERIES

Book 1
Lady's Big Surprise
Hardback ISBN-13: 978-0-9746561-5-1
Paperback ISBN-13: 978-0-9746561-6-8

Book 2
Star of Wonder
Hardback ISBN-13: 978-0-9746561-3-7
Paperback ISBN-13: 978-0-9746561-4-4

Book 3
Willie to the Rescue
Hardback ISBN-13: 978-0-9746561-0-6
Paperback ISBN-13: 978-0-9746561-2-0

Book 4
Mary and Jody in the Movies
Hardback ISBN-13: 978-0-9746561-1-3
Paperback ISBN-13: 978-0-9746561-9-9

Are you a fan of the
Lucky Foot Stable
Series?

**Get a signed PHOTO of the author with
her horse, Painted Warrior!**

... when you join The Lucky Foot Stable Fan Club.

Here's your chance to keep up on the latest news and merchandise,
chat with other fans, and have the opportunity to visit
Tailwinds Farm, home and riding stable of JoAnn S. Dawson.

Become a member now!
Go to www.luckyfootseries.com

Happy Reading and Riding!